White Nights

Alina Doris

Contents

Chapter 1 - Mr. Arrogant

Sarah's POV

I grabbed my coffee and walked out of the cafe quickly. I was late.

Suddenly, I bumped into someone. He caught me by my waist quickly, saving me from falling. The coffee cup fell down. I placed my hands on his firm chest. Our eyes met. He had captivating green eyes. It seemed like time stopped. We were staying here, staring at each other.

"Sorry." I murmured.

The corner of his lips curled up.

"It was pleasure for me." He said in his husky accented voice, giving me an arrogant smirk.

I straightened. He was staring at me with an arrogant smirk.

He wore a dark gray shirt and black jeans. He was so handsome and sexy.

"Next time be careful, kiska. (kitty)" He warned arrogantly. He winked at me and walked away.

I was staying in the same place, dumbfounded. I pulled myself together and went towards my car.

As I arrived at the company, I went to my father's office. I walked towards the secretary.

"Good morning, Ava. Is my father in his office?" I asked.

"Good morning, Ms. Miller. Yes, he is." She replied, giving me a slight smile.

I nodded and went towards the office. I knocked on the door and opened the door. I walked in and closed the door behind me.

"Good morning." I greeted them happily.

My brother, Ethan was here, too. I hugged my father, then my brother.

"Princess, are you ready?" My father asked.

My father and I were going to go to Russia tomorrow. We were going to have a meeting with a Russian businessman about a project in St. Petersburg.

"Yes, I packed my suitcase." I replied.

"Great, we will leave in five minutes. The jet is waiting for us." He informed; I nodded.

The jet landed in Russia. We went to the hotel. This evening we were having dinner with the Russian businessman.

I put on my black mini dress. I left my hair open. I took my clutch and left the suite. My father was waiting for me in the lobby.

We went towards the restaurant. A man, about in his early fifties, stood up, smiling at us. We walked towards him. My father shook his hand.

"Welcome. Nice to see you again. And you must be Sarah. You are so beautiful, daughter. My name is Sergei. Nice to meet you." He said, shaking my hand, smiling at me warmly.

"Thank you. Nice to meet you. " I gave him a polite smile.

We sat down and ordered our meals.

"My son will join us. He is about to arrive." He informed.

"How is Dimitri?" My father asked.

"As always." He replied, shaking his head. My father gave him a smile.

"I am sorry that I was late."

I heard a familiar voice. I lifted my head up and looked at him. I was surprised. It was him. The stranger in front of the cafe. He looked so handsome in his suit.

He shook my father's hand without noticing me.

"Dimitri, let me introduce you to Sarah Miller, Peter's daughter. Sarah, he is my son, Dimitri." Sergei introduced.

Dimitri looked at me. When he remembered me, the corner of his lips curled up. He extended his hand to me, smirking arrogantly.

"Nice to meet you, Sarah." He said.

I shook his hand, nodding. When I wanted to pull my hand away, he held my hand tightly.

Then, we sat down. He was staring at me. I was not looking at him anymore, but I felt his eyes on me.

"Dima." A blonde woman called him, walking towards our table.

She wore an ultra mini white dress.

She wrapped his arms around Dimitri's neck from behind, showing her white teeth. She kissed his lips. He pulled his head away quickly.

"Alyona? What are you doing here?" He asked, annoyed and stood up.

"You did not pick up my call. So I called your secretary, she told me you were here." She replied. Then she traveled her gaze from Dimitri to us. "Good evening." She greeted.

"Good evening." My father said. I nodded.

His father cleared his throat without greeting her. He looked angry.

"Sorry. I will come back." Dimitri stated and walked away, dragging the woman with him by her arm.

Suddenly, my phone rang.

"Excuse me." I said and stood up, picking up my phone.

I went to the lobby. After talking on the phone, I saw Dimitri and the girl arguing.

"Хватит!" (Enough!) He shouted, running his hand through his hair, frustrated.

The girl scowled at him and walked away angrily.

Dimitri walked towards the restaurant.

When he saw me, he walked closer to me. His face expression changed. His arrogant smirk appeared on his face. He put his hands into his pocket.

"Are you spying on me, kiska?" He asked, giving me a mischievous smirk.

I narrowed my eyes at him. "Of course not . Why do I need to spy on you and your girlfriend?!" I replied, folding my arms over my chest.

He burst out laughing. A dazzling laugh.

"Ex-girlfriend." He corrected and walked into the restaurant without waiting for me.

Ugh! Jerk!

After dinner, we left the restaurant.

"Ok then, See you tomorrow. We will talk about the details in the meeting tomorrow." Sergei told us.

"See you tomorrow." My father said and shook his hand.

Then he shook my hand. After Dimitri shook my father's hand, my father and Sergei walked away a little, talking.

"Good night, kiska." Dimitri said, smirking playfully. He winked at me and joined his father.

After saying goodbye, they left. I went to my suite. I was tired. I put on my lace nightie and went to bed.

Suddenly, I heard a knock on the door.

Who was this?

Probably, it was my father. I got up and put on my silk robe. I walked towards the door and opened it.

Dimitri was standing in front of me, his signature smirk on his face, his hands in his pockets. He roamed my body from head to toe, biting his lower lip.

A few seconds later, I found myself between the wall and his body. He was looking at me lustfully.

I placed my hands on his firm chest. My heartbeats fastened. There were a few inches between our lips. He moved his gaze from my eyes to my lips. He cupped my cheek and brushed his lips against mine, kissing me in a possessive and passionate kiss.

Chapter 2 - Magic

- -

S arah's POV

I felt butterflies in my stomach. He tightened his arm around me, kissing me passionately. I responded to his kiss, moving my hands up along his chest.

He pulled my lower lip between his teeth and pulled back a little, looking into my eyes full of passion in his eyes.

"Put your clothes on! You are coming with me. I will show you magic." He demanded huskily.

"Hmm?" I looked at him, dumbfounded.

He smirked arrogantly. "Do you want to stay here...and continue what we have started, kiska?" He asked with a cocky grin.

I narrowed my eyes at him. He chuckled and pulled away.

"Hurry up!" He ordered.

"I am not coming with you anywhere." I protested, folding my arms over my chest.

He walked closer to me, trailing his fingertip along my cheek, sending shivers down my spine.

"Do not worry I will not eat you...tonight." He murmured in my ear huskily and pulled back, grinning; I gave him a dirty look. He chuckled.

"Come on."

"Ok. Wait here." I sighed as I accepted and went to the bedroom.

I put on blue jeans and a white blouse. I took my bag and left the bedroom.

"I am ready." I informed.

"Great! Let's go."

He held my hand quickly and dragged me out with him without letting me protest.

When we walked out of the hotel, the sky was not dark, despite the fact that it was midnight.

"I told you I would show you magic." He murmured in my ear; I looked at him, puzzled.

"White nights. You can see this only in St. Petersburg. From late May to early July, the nights are bright here. It stands at such a high latitude that the sun does not descend below the horizon enough for the sky to grow dark." He explained with a serious expression.

"It is beautiful." I commented, looking around in awe.

He smiled, placing his hand on my lower back as he headed me towards a black Lamborghini.

We got in his car. He started the car.

I was staring at him. He was so handsome with his blond hair and green eyes. And his charming smile.

He turned his head towards me and gave me a bright smile.

He parked his car as we arrived at our destination. We got out of the car. In front of us was the Neva River.

We leaned against the trunk hood, watching the magical scenery in front of us. Dimitri was giving me information about here.

We were watching the raising of the drawbridges across the Neva River. This was the signature tradition of the White Nights: watching the spectacle of the massive Neva River bridges heaving apart to let through boat traffic. The most popular spot, which offered the best views of the Palace and Trinity bridges going up. There was a carnival atmosphere, with bands playing nearby, food and drink stalls and party boats going up and down the river.

I listened to him, memorizing his gestures, voice and face.

"What are you thinking about?" He asked, interrupting my thoughts.

I turned my head towards him. "About why I am here, despite your annoying arrogance." I admitted honestly.

He chuckled. "You are here despite my annoying arrogance. If you like me more, think what will happen then." He commented arrogantly and chuckled, emphasizing the words, annoying arrogance.

"You are getting into deep water." I warned, raising my eyebrow.

"Then save me." He said, leaning closer to me.

He stroked my cheek with his fingertip, increasing my heartbeats.

We met a few hours ago, but his effect on me was undeniable.

He kissed my lips softly, wrapping his arm around me, his other hand was resting on my cheek. He pulled me closer to him as he deepened the kiss.

I stood up and wrapped my arms around his neck without separating our lips. I was standing between his legs. He pressed his bulge into my stomach while holding me still against his body. He was devouring my mouth with his skillful mouth and tongue.

Our soft kiss became rough.

A few minutes later, we pulled back to catch our breaths.

"What are you doing to me, kiska?" He murmured, stroking my cheek while panting.

He wrapped his arms around me, resting his head on my shoulder, hugging me tightly. I hugged him back.

"Don't you think we are going too fast?" I asked, still in his arms.

"I like speeding things up. Slowness is too boring for me." He winked at me and placed a soft kiss on my lips.

I woke up, feeling happy the following morning. I got up and went to the bathroom.

After taking a shower, I put on a black pencil skirt and a blush pink blouse. I took my bag and left.

My father was waiting for me in the lobby. We went to the company.

Sergei greeted us. I saw Dimitri faraway walking towards us, his hands in his pockets. He looked so handsome in his black suit.

When he noticed us, he smiled at me while walking towards us. He greeted us as he approached us.

We went to the conference room. I felt his gaze on me.

When I looked at him, he winked at me. I turned my gaze away, biting my lower lip.

After the meeting, I went to the hotel. My father and Sergei stayed in the company.

I changed my clothes and lay down on the bed.

Suddenly, my phone buzzed. I grabbed my phone and looked at the screen.

'What about dinner? Dimitri.'

I smiled happily. 'OK.'

I sent him a message. My phone buzzed again.

'Great! I will pick you up at 6.00 p.m.'

I put my phone down on the bed and got up to choose a dress for dinner; I was so excited.

I wore a silver mini dress. I looked at myself in the mirror and took my clutch.

Dimitri was waiting for me in front of the hotel, leaning against his car.

When he saw me, he straightened, staring at me from head to toe lustfully. I walked towards him.

"Good evening." I greeted him.

"Good evening. You are so beautiful." He murmured, wrapping his arm around me, kissing my lips. Then, he pulled back.

"Let's go, kiska." He suggested; I nodded.

He opened the door for me. I got in the car as I thanked him. Then he got in his car, too and started the car.

He stopped his car in front of the luxurious restaurant. We got out of the car. He gave the key to the valet and placed his hand on my back protectively as we walked in.

Chapter 3 - The gentleman

S arah's POV

After having dinner, we went to the nightclub. Dimitri placed his hand on my lower back as we walked in. There were a lot of people.

He placed his hand on my back, pulling me closer to him.

"Would you like some drink?" He asked.

"Yes, Cosmo, please!"

He nodded and went towards the bar counter.

We were talking, drinking.

"Dance with me." He extended his hand towards me.

I held his hand, and we walked towards the dance floor. He wrapped his arms around my waist, pulling me closer to him.

I leaned my head against his chest. His breath fanned against my neck, sending shivers down my spine.

Dimitri's POV

Sarah placed her empty glass down on the table and mumbled. "Another Cosmo...please."

She was drunk.

"This is enough for tonight. Let's go." I demanded, wrapping my arm around her waist.

"No, I want to drink." She pouted.

"No." I protested confidently.

After I had helped her to get in the car, I got in the car, too and started the car. She was staring at me while grinning at me sheepishly. Drunk and cute. I smiled.

I stopped the car in front of the hotel. I got out of the car and opened the door for her. She got out of the car. She wrapped her arms around my neck, giggling.

"Why did you not tell me you have a twin?" She asked. She was barely standing on her feet.

I wrapped my arm around her waist.

"What?" I asked, raising my eyebrow.

"But I prefer you." She said, giggling; I smiled.

"Side effects of Cosmo, kiska." I commented, grinning.

She giggled and pulled my arm away. "I can walk myself."

When she was falling down, I caught her by her waist quickly. I scooped her up in my arms bridal style. She wrapped her arms around my neck, placing her head on my shoulder. I carried her to her suite.

I closed the door behind us with my foot. I set her on her feet. I took my jacket off and placed it in the armchair.

"You need to sleep. Let me help you." I offered.

"No. I do not want to sleep." She pouted and pushed me back onto the couch.

She giggled, looking at me lustfully and took off her dress. She was freaking sexy. I felt my member getting hard.

Fuck!

She sat on my lap and started kissing my lips. She wrapped her hands around my neck, kissing me passionately.

A few seconds later, I responded to her kiss, wrapping my arms around her waist, kissing her passionately. She took off my tie, pressing herself against my member. I groaned.

The corner of her lips curled up. She was unbuttoning my shirt. I pulled back and grabbed her hands. She looked at me, puzzled.

"Not tonight, kiska. You are drunk. I want you sober when you scream my name under me." I stated confidently, looking into her eyes.

I wrapped my arm around her waist and stood up, pulling her with me. I scooped her up in my arms and carried her to the bed. I placed her on the bed carefully. She looked into my eyes, lying on the bed only in her lace underwear.

"I am falling in love with you." She murmured.

My eyes lit up. I stared at her.

"Good night, kiska." I said huskily.

She closed her eyes slowly. I pulled a blanket over her. I went towards the other side of the bed as I took my shoes off and lay down beside her on the bed. She rolled over and wrapped her arm around my waist, placing her head on my chest, her eyes still closed. I wrapped my arms around her, hugging her tightly. I placed a soft kiss on her hair before closing my eyes.

Sarah's POV

I felt strong arms wrapped around me. I opened my eyes. Dimitri was sleeping, hugging me tightly. I was only in my underwear. I remembered last night. I felt embarrassed.

How will I look him in his eyes?

I stroked his cheek. He sighed but did not wake up.

When I wanted to pull back, he opened his eyes.

"Morning, kiska." He said in a sleepy voice.

"Good morning." I murmured without looking into his eyes. "Sorry for last night....And thank you." I muttered, blushing.

He placed his finger under my chin and lifted my head up, letting our eyes meet. He leaned over and brushed his lips against mine, his arms still wrapped around me. Then, he pulled back, placing his hand on my cheek.

"Do not worry. You can drink as much as you want if I am beside you. But only beside me, kiska. Get it?" He stated with a serious expression. I nodded.

"Great!" He exclaimed, giving me a tender smile.

I got up and put on my silk robe. He got up and approached me. He wrapped his arms around me.

"It is not your fault that you wanted to jump on me. It is the effects of my irresistible charm." He commented with a mischievous smirk on his face.

I raised my eyebrow at him. He chuckled.

"And it is good to know that you want me because I want you so badly." He murmured in my ear huskily, pressing his member into my stomach.

I felt so hot. His breath fanned my neck. I bit my lower lip.

"Next time you will moan under me in pleasure." He promised and kissed my lips.

I wrapped my arms around his neck as I responded to his kiss. He slid his hand under my robe, stroking my thigh. I moaned into his mouth. The corner of his lips curled up. He cupped my cheek, kissing me roughly.

He pulled back, leaning his forehead against mine.

"See you later, kiska." He said as he pulled back.

He put his tie into his pocket and grabbed his jacket. He winked at me and left the suite, leaving me with a hot desire for him.

Chapter 4 - Nightmare

Dimitri's POV

"No...Don't go!....Don't leave me!" I woke up, screaming.

I was drenched in sweat. I sat up and ran my hand through my hair.

It was 6.00 a.m. I got up and went to the bathroom.

After taking a shower, I put on sweatpants, a white shirt and a hoodie. I grabbed my phone; I wanted to call Sarah. I needed to hear her voice. But I gave up; it was too early. Probably, she was sleeping. I placed my phone down on the bedside table.

I went to the kitchen and made some coffee for myself. I was sipping my coffee, looking out of the window, my hand in my pocket.

"Dima, are you fine?" Galina's voice interrupted my thoughts. I did not hear when she came.

Galina was my housekeeper. She took care of us: my sister and me. She was in her late forties. She was caring and kind. I really loved her. She was like a mother to me.

I turned around.

"Yes." I murmured and continued staring out.

"A nightmare again?" She asked sadly. I did not answer.

"I will make breakfast for you." She informed softly.

"No, I do not want to. Thank you." I said, placing the cup down on the table and went to my room.

I changed my clothes. I wanted to see Sarah.

I grabbed my phone and left.

Sarah's POV

I got up and went to the bathroom.

After taking a shower, I put on black jeans and a horizontally striped shirt. I did my hair wavy.

My phone rang. It was Dimitri. I picked up the phone, excited.

"Good morning." I greeted him happily.

"Good morning. How are you?" He asked huskily. His voice was gloomy.

"Fine. And you?" I asked, concerned.

"I am fine. Thanks. I am in front of the hotel, waiting for you." He informed.

"Ok. I am coming." I said and hung up.

I grabbed my bag and left.

As I approached him, he hugged me tightly. I hugged him back.

Dimitri pulled back, stroking my cheek and placed a soft kiss on my lips. Then he held my hand and headed us towards his car. He opened the door for me. I got in the car. He got in the car and started the car.

He pulled the car over.

"Wait for me here." He demanded and got out of the car without letting me say anything.

A few minutes later, he came with two bicycles. I got out of the car and gave him a wide smile.

Dimitri and I started riding our bicycles. We had fun like children.

After having dinner together, we went back to my hotel. He accompanied me to my suite as always.

We were in the elevator. I was looking at changing floor numbers. I felt his eyes on me. I bit my lower lip nervously.

Suddenly, he pushed me back to the wall and smashed his lips against mine, pinning me up against the wall. I wrapped my arms around him. He slid his hand under my shirt while he was devouring my mouth with his tongue. He trailed his lips down to my neck, cupping my cheek. He bit my neck slightly. I groaned, pulling his hair slightly.

Suddenly, the door opened. Dimitri pulled back instantly. He held my hand and headed us to my suite, taking quick steps.

As soon as he closed the door behind us, he pressed me against the wall, claiming my lips roughly. I ran my hands through his hair. He pulled my lower lip between his teeth, making me moan.

Dimitri took my shirt off and threw it away, moving his lips down to my neck, to my breast, to my stomach. I arched my back, moaning. He moved his lips up and kissed my lips while he was cupping my breast. I unbuttoned his shirt and took it off. He unclasped my bra. I moved my hands along his bare back. He placed kisses along my jawline, pulling my nipple between his thumb and index finger. I moaned louder, gripping his hair. He moved his lips down to my breasts and sucked my nipple while he was cupping my breast.

Dimitri straightened and kissed my lips while he was unzipping my fly. He took my jeans off and claimed my lips. I ran my hands through his hair. He squeezed my butt, making me gasp. He took advantage of it and plunged his tongue into my mouth. I was melting under his expert touches. He lifted me up, still kissing me. I wrapped my legs around his waist.

He carried me to my bedroom and put me on the bed. He crawled on the bed and kissed my lips, sliding his hand under my lace panties. I shivered under him. He moved his lips down to my breasts, to my stomach, placing soft kisses. He took my panties off and threw it away. He spread my legs apart and started kissing me between my legs. I shivered, squeezing my eyes shut.

"Dimitri." I moaned in ecstasy.

He was teasing me with his tongue. I shuddered, coming. He got up and took his clothes off. He positioned himself between my legs and shoved his length inside me. I gasped, screaming in pain, squeezing my eyes shut. He froze.

"You..." He murmured. I nodded.

"Please, continue. " I murmured shyly. He nodded and started thrusting.

"Oh...you...are....so...tight...kiska. It...feels...so...good." He murmured between his thrusts.

Dimitri kissed my lips while he was thrusting inside me faster and harder, making me come again and again. Then he came inside me and collapsed on top of me.

We were panting. He rolled over and pulled me into his embrace. He placed a soft kiss on my forehead.

"Did I hurt you so much?" He asked, concerned.

"No. Don't worry." I replied, blushing.

He smiled, stroking my cheek and placed a soft kiss on my lips. I placed my head on his chest.

He was running his fingertip along my bare back. I smiled. He kissed my hair, hugging me tightly.

"Good night, kiska." He said.

"Good night." I murmured and closed my eyes.

Chapter 5 - The unpleasant encounter

S arah's POV

When I opened my eyes, my eyes met a pair of beautiful green eyes. Dimitri was staring at me, playing with a lock of my hair.

"Good morning, kiska." He said huskily, stroking my hair.

"Good morning." I gave him a radiant smile, stroking his cheek.

Dimitri held my hand and kissed my palm. He tightened his arms around me, pulling me into his chest and kissed my lips.

I was on top of him now. I cupped his cheeks, kissing him back. He moved his hand down along my bare body, pressing his bulge against my stomach. A little groan escaped from my mouth.

Our kiss was getting more passionate. He moved his hand down between my legs and pushed his two fingers inside me. I gasped, gripping his shoulders. He was kissing me roughly while his fingers were torturing me. He pulled his fingers out, leaving me empty. He lifted me up by my hips and slammed his length inside me.

I arched my back, moaning and started moving, placing my hands on his firm chest. He placed his hands on my hips, controlling my pace.

Our moans filled the room. He sat up and wrapped his arms around me, thrusting inside me roughly while kissing my neck. I gripped his hair, closing my eyes shut.

A few thrusts later, we came together, screaming each other's name out. I collapsed on his chest. He wrapped his arms around me and pulled his length out of me.

I was still on top of him. He was stroking my hair.

When I opened my eyes, I was still laying on top of him.

Dimitri was sleeping peacefully; his arms wrapped around me. I kissed his lips, stroking his hair. He sighed, but he did not wake up. I buried my head into the crook of his neck, lying in silence, breathing his musky scent.

He blinked and opened his eyes. He smiled at me, kissing my hair.

"It feels good holding you in my arms." He murmured, tightening his arms around me, trailing his nose along my cheek.

"It feels good being in your arms." I confessed, kissing his lips. "But I need to take a shower." I added.

He nodded as he said. "I will order breakfast while you are taking a shower."

I nodded in agreement. He released me, letting me get up. I got up and went to the bathroom.

After taking a shower, I wrapped the towel around me and walked out. Dimitri was talking on the phone, only in his boxers. I was staring at him, biting my lower lip. He was so sexy. I remembered his kisses, his touches.

He hung up and turned around. He roamed me from head to toe lustfully. He approached me and trailed his fingertip down from my cheek to my neck, to my arm. I closed my eyes as my body shivered in sensation.

What is he doing to me?

I couldn't control my body beside him.

"They brought breakfast. I will take a quick shower." He informed huskily and kissed my lips.

I put on a black skirt and a white tank top.

I was starving.

Dimitri walked out of the bathroom, a towel wrapped around his waist. I felt an uncomfortable sensation between my legs. I bit my lower lip, staring at him.

He smirked and walked towards me. He cupped my cheeks in his hands, caressing my cheeks with his thumbs.

"I like when you are blushing." He murmured in my ear and placed a soft kiss on my neck.

He put on his boxer and pants. He held my hand and headed us to the other room. We had breakfast together.

He was putting his shirt on in front of the mirror. I walked closer to him and wrapped my arms around him from behind, leaning my head against his back. He placed his hand on top of my hands and entwined our fingers.

He turned around and wrapped his arms around me. I trailed my hands on his bare chest. He closed his eyes.

When he opened his eyes, he was looking into my eyes lustfully.

"Let me button your shirt up." I murmured; he nodded without taking his eyes off me.

I started buttoning up his shirt. He was staring at me.

"Done." I pulled back, smiling.

"Thank you." He said, stroking my cheek. "See you later, kiska." He added and kissed my lips.

"See you later."

He winked at me and left.

I woke up with my phone ringtone. I grabbed my phone. There was a message from Dimitri.

'Good morning, kiska. Miss you.'

I smiled as I read his message.

'Good morning. Miss you, too.'

I sent it and put my phone down on the bedside table. I got up and went to the bathroom.

After taking a shower, I wrapped the towel around me and walked out of the bathroom.

I put on a navy blue dress and did my hair.

Today Dimitri was busy. I decided to go shopping.

After having breakfast with my father, I went to my suite. I took my bag and left.

I got out of the taxi in front of the shopping mall. After finishing shopping, I decided to go to the cafe at the mall; I was tired, and I wanted to drink something.

When I walked into the cafe, I saw Dimitri at the cafe.

He was talking to a blond woman. I couldn't see her face. Her back was turned to me. They were talking, laughing.

The woman stroked his cheek. He put his hand on top of her hand on the table, smiling at her.

I felt dizzy. My legs were frozen. I couldn't breathe anymore.

Suddenly, a little girl ran towards him. Dimitri smiled at the little girl and picked up her, placing her on his lap.

He tickled the little girl, making her giggle. The little girl had light brown hair with a pair of green eyes. A pair of familiar green eyes like Dimitri's.

I gasped.

No! No! No!

My legs were trembling. I looked at them. They were laughing happily. I placed my hand on the wall for support.

Chapter 6 - Misunderstanding

Sarah's POV

A few seconds later, the woman stood up and walked towards the restroom.

My eyes filled with tears. He was playing with me. I believed him like a fool. I couldn't breathe anymore.

When I turned around to leave, Dimitri called my name behind me. I turned around. Our eyes met. He was looking at me, surprised. He stood up and set the little girl on her feet.

I walked towards them in slow steps. He smiled at me. He walked closer to me and wrapped his arm around my waist, kissing my cheek.

"What are you doing here, kiska?" He asked.

Is it a joke?!

I looked at him, full of anger and disappointment in my eyes. I pulled back. He looked at me, puzzled.

The little girl walked towards us, looking at me. She stopped beside Dimitri. I was looking at her. She was so beautiful and cute.

"Дядя, кто она?" She asked him something in Russian.

"Одну минуту, принцесса." He replied, stroking her hair. She nodded, giving him an innocent smile.

"Are you fine, kiska? Your face is pale." He said, concerned, placing his hand on my arm.

I pulled my arm away.

Suddenly, my head spun. He caught me by my waist quickly.

"Sarah!" He placed his hand on my cheek.

"Bring some water!" He ordered a waiter.

"Come. Sit down." He helped me sit down.

The waiter brought a glass of water for me. Dimitri grabbed the glass and extended it to me. I took it with my trembling hands.

"Are you better now?" He asked and bent down beside me.

"Yes...Sorry for disturbing your family time. Your daughter is waiting for you." I murmured dryly. He looked at me, puzzled.

"My daughter?" He asked with questioning eyes, raising his eyebrow.

A few seconds later, the corner of his lips curled up. He straightened, smirking.

"Let me introduce you to my niece, Karina." He stated, smirking.

I looked at him, dumbfounded.

His niece?

"Karina, meet my girlfriend, Sarah." He said, emphasizing the words my girlfriend, stroking the little girl's hair while looking into my eyes.

"Hi." The little girl greeted me, giving me a shy smile.

"Hi." I mumbled, smiling at her, still in shock.

"Dima?" I heard a woman's voice coming behind me.

I turned towards her.

She had a pair of green eyes. The same shade as Dimitri and little girl's. She looked like Dimitri.

"Valentina, let me introduce you to Sarah. She is my girlfriend. Sarah, this is Valentina, my sister." Dimitri introduced.

My cheeks turned crimson red. I stood up.

"Nice to meet you, dear. Dimitri talked about you a lot." She said happily and hugged me. I hugged her back, embarrassed.

"Nice to meet you, too." I mumbled, giving her a slight smile.

"Are you okay, dear?" She asked me, concerned.

"Yeah, I am." I murmured.

Dimitri chuckled. I couldn't look him in his eyes.

Stupid Sarah!

"Umm..I need to go...See you later." I said.

"See you later, dear." She gave me a broad smile.

"I am coming." Dimitri informed his sister. She nodded.

He placed his hand on my lower back and headed us towards the exit.

"Sorry." I murmured.

He placed his hand on my cheek and stroked it.

"It is great to know that you are jealous." He commented huskily, caressing my cheek with his thumb. I blushed.

He leaned closer to me and captured my lips. He wrapped his arm around my waist, pulling me closer to him, cupping my cheek. I moved my hand up from his chest to his neck while kissing him.

He pulled back. "You are mine tonight. Be ready at 7.00 o'clock." He stated huskily. I nodded.

Dimitri's POV

After Sarah had left, I walked back. I was so happy; she was jealous. I couldn't stop myself from smiling.

I sat down on the seat next to Valentina.

"She is beautiful." My sister commented, giving me a knowing smile. I smirked.

"Yes, she is." I agreed.

"Aww. My little brother is in love. Finally! I was about to lose my hope." She commented, placing her hand on top of my hand on the table, giving me an impish smile. I chuckled.

Sarah's POV

After taking a shower, I put on a black mini dress. I left my hair open. I took my clutch and went downstairs. Dimitri was waiting for me in front of the hotel.

He wore a white shirt and black jeans. He looked so handsome.

When he saw me, he looked at me from head to toe. He wrapped his arm around me as he approached me and pulled me into his chest. He brushed his lips against mine. I wrapped my arms around his neck as I responded to his kiss.

He pulled back and leaned his forehead against mine.

"You are so beautiful." He murmured.

"Thank you."

He pulled back and opened the door for me. I got in the car. He got in the car and started driving.

After having dinner, he said he had a surprise for me.

He pulled his car over as we arrived at our destination. We got out of the car. He approached me and pulled a silk scarf out of his pocket.

"Turn around and close your eyes." He demanded huskily.

I turned around without protesting. I was wondering what was his surprise. I closed my eyes. He covered my eyes with the scarf. He wrapped his arm around me and helped me to walk.

We walked into somewhere. Car noises stopped. A few minutes later, the wind was blowing through my hair.

"Are you ready? " He murmured in my ear.

"Yes." I replied in excitement.

He uncovered my eyes; I opened my eyes. We were on the roof.

"Dimitri!" I exclaimed in awe; the incredible and luminous view of the city's canals and rivers was in front of us. Like the city was at our feet.

There was a blanket on the floor and a bottle of wine and two glasses on it. He wrapped his arms around my waist from behind.

"You....I...the sky...and...a bottle of wine." He murmured in my ear, emphasizing each word, placing kisses on my neck.

I turned around and wrapped my arms around his neck.

"I... like...you...I...the sky...and...a bottle of wine." I stated, emphasizing each word, between placing kisses on his lips.

We were sitting on the blanket, drinking and talking. Then, we lay down on the blanket and started watching the sky.

He leaned on his elbow, running his fingertip along my cheek. I turned my eyes towards him. He was looking at me with salacious eyes. He leaned over me and captured my lips. I wrapped my arms around his neck, pulling him closer to me. He moved his lips down to my neck, kissing my neck while he removed the strap of my dress.

I placed my head on his bare chest, only in his shirt. He wrapped his arm around me and placed a kiss on my hair.

***

"Дядя, кто она?" - "Uncle, who is she?"

"Одну минуту, принцесса." - "One minute, princess."

Chapter 7 – Distracting

Sarah's POV

I heard a knock on the door. I walked towards the door and opened it.

"Hi, kiska."

This was Dimitri. He wore a khaki hoodie and black jeans. We were going camping today.

He wrapped his arm around me and kissed my lips.

"Are you ready?" He asked.

"Yeah." I replied, giving him a bright smile.

I took my bag, and we left.

He stopped the car at our destination. We got out of the car.

We were going camping at Lake Ladoga.

We swam, talked. At night, Dimitri and I fell asleep in the tent, hugging each other.

Today, we were going back. Watching the luminous sky across the infinite horizon of this vast lake from beside a campfire was an unforgettable experience. And of course, being with Dimitri.

He dropped me off at my hotel. As soon as I arrived, I took a shower.

Today, my father and I had a meeting.

I put on a bold blue blouse and a black skirt. I took my bag and left my suite. I went to the company with my father.

We were in the conference room. Dimitri was here, too. He was sitting beside me. He wore a navy blue suit, a white shirt and a blue tie. He was so handsome as always. I couldn't take my eyes off him.

He placed his hand on my thigh without drawing attention, sliding his hand under my skirt, while he was listening to his father with a serious expression on his face. He was moving his hand up and down slowly. I placed my hand on top of his hand and pulled his hand away as I gave him a warning look.

After the meeting, we went to his father's room, but Dimitri did not join us.

My phone buzzed. I pulled my phone out of my bag. It was Dimitri.

'Come to my office.'

I put my phone back into my bag and stood up.

"Excuse me, I need to use the restroom." I lied and left the room.

I knocked on his door and opened the door.

Dimitri was watching out, his hands in his pockets. I walked in and closed the door behind me. He gave me a mischievous smirk as he approached me, looking at me lustfully.

"Do you know how much your skirt is distracting?" He murmured seductively, stroking my cheek. I bit my lower lip shyly.

He pushed me back against the wall and captured my lips. I ran my hands through his hair. He unbuttoned my blouse, moving his lips to my neck, to my breast while he was stroking my thigh.

"Dimitri." I murmured in ecstasy.

I hated his effect on my body.

Dimitri slipped his two fingers under my panties. I moaned, gripping his hair as he pushed his fingers inside me. I squeezed my lips together, trying not to moan loudly. He was moving his fingers in and out while he was cupping, kissing my breast. Then he turned me around.

"Put your hands on the wall." He demanded huskily.

I placed my hands on the wall. He pulled my panties down.

A few seconds later, he was inside me. I groaned. He wrapped his arm around me, thrusting inside me roughly. I was squeezing my lips together not to moan. He was cupping my breast while thrusting inside me harder and deeply. My legs were trembling in sensation. I moaned, coming. A few thrusts later, he came inside me. We were panting.

I was adjusting my clothes. Meanwhile, he was staring at me with sparkling eyes.

"You are mine today. I am waiting for you in the parking lot." He informed huskily without taking his eyes off on me.

"My father...Ok." I murmured.

He gave me a charming smile. I left his office.

I told my father that I was going to meet up with my friend.

Dimitri was waiting for me, leaning against his car. He opened his door for me. I got in the car. He closed the door for me and got in the car, too.

"Where are we going?" I asked.

"Surprise." He replied and winked at me.

He parked his car in front of the building and got out of his car. He opened the door for me and offered his hand. I gave my hand and got out of the car. He headed me towards the elevator. He entered the password.

The door opened, and we walked into the penthouse.

"Welcome to my home." He murmured in my ear with an amused expression, wrapping his arm around my waist.

The home was dramatically contemporary, with warm, comfortable, open living spaces, soaring ceilings and walls of glass that offer breathtaking views. Replete with lush, smoked ebony floors, rich walnut walls, a fabulous kitchen, and a terrace that surrounded the entire residence offering spectacular views of the city. Unique design features include a custom-built, lighted wall sculpture over the living room fireplace.

"It is so beautiful." I commented.

"Would you like to drink some wine? Red or white?" He asked, taking his jacket and tie off.

"Red, please." I replied and sat down on the couch.

He walked towards the kitchen and came back with two glasses of red wine. He handed me the glass.

"Thank you." I took it and sipped my wine.

"Are you hungry? I am going to make spaghetti Bolognese for you." He said, giving me a bright smile.

I nodded, smiling. He got up and held my hand, heading us towards the kitchen.

I was staring at him. He was moving in the kitchen gracefully while he was making our dinner.

He extended the spoon towards me. I opened my mouth and tasted it. I closed my eyes.

"It is delicious." I commented in awe. He smirked.

"I know." He winked at me.

"What will I do with your arrogance?" I asked playfully.

"Hmm...We can find something." He replied, giving me a seductive smirk. I shook my head, smiling.

"You are hopeless." I commented, smiling. He raised his eyebrow at me and walked closer to me.

"I thought you loved me like I am." He stated and started tickling me, laughing happily.

"Stop, Dimitri!" I exclaimed, laughing, but he didn't obey.

A few minutes later, he stopped and placed a soft kiss on my lip.

After eating dinner, we watched a movie together.

I yawned. I was tired.

"Are you tired?" He asked, stroking my hair. I nodded.

"Let's go to bed then." He got up and held my hand, heading us to his bedroom.

I changed my clothes. I wore his shirt; it covered my thigh barely.

He was laying on the bed, staring at me.

"I like my clothes on you." He confessed without taking his eyes off my bare legs.

I lay down on the bed and hugged him. He wrapped his arm around me tightly.

"Goodnight, kiska." He placed a soft kiss on my hair.

"Goodnight." I said and closed my eyes, breathing his scent.

Chapter 8 - Haunted

S arah's POV

I was woken up by Dimitri's voice.

"No!...Don't go!"

He was drenched in sweat. He was twisting in the bed, murmuring something. I shook his shoulder.

"Dimitri! Wake up!" I shook him again. He opened his eyes, breathing deeply.

"It is okay. It was a nightmare." I assured him.

He pulled me into his lap, hugging me tightly, burying his head into the crook of my neck. I stroked his hair, trying to calm him down.

I pulled back a little, cupping his cheek.

"Are you better now?" I asked, concerned. He nodded.

"Do you want to tell me about your nightmare?" I asked.

He shook his head without saying anything.

"Ok." I said, hugging him.

We were laying on the bed in silence. He placed his head on my chest, hugging me tightly like his life depended on me. I was stroking his hair.

When I woke up, the sun was shining through the window. I looked at Dimitri, who was sleeping beside me peacefully, his arm around me. I stroked his cheek and placed a tender kiss on his cheek. He sighed but did not wake up. I pulled his hand away carefully without waking him up and got up. I went to the bathroom and took a shower.

I wrapped the towel around me and walked out of the bathroom. Dimitri was awake. He looked at me from head to toe, his hands under his head.

"Morning." He said huskily.

"Good morning. How are you?" I asked. He looked at me tenderly.

"I am fine. Do not worry. And sorry for last night." He gave me an apologetic look.

Dimitri got up and walked closer to me. He wrapped his arm around me, pulling me closer, inhaling my scent.

"I like when you smell like me." He murmured, trailing his lips along my neck. I closed my eyes in sensation.

"It..is..your...body shower." I muttered.

Dimitri was still moving his lips along my neck without kissing me. He moved his hands down to my thighs and rubbed them. Then he bit my neck, making me moan.

"Dimitri." I murmured.

He pulled back and kissed my lips. I ran my hand through his hair. He lifted me up, still kissing me passionately. I wrapped my legs around his waist.

Dimitri carried me to the bed and put me on the bed. He leaned over and claimed my lips again while he was removing my towel. He moved his lips down to my breast while he was cupping my other breast. He moved his hand down and pushed his two fingers inside me, making me gasp. I ran my hand through his hair, pressing my head back.

A few seconds later, his tongue joined his fingers. I moaned. He was torturing me with his skillful fingers.

"Dimitri...please...." I murmured, shivering.

"What, kiska? What do you want?" He asked huskily.

"You." I replied.

He smirked at me and got up, taking his clothes off. He grasped my ankles in one hand, pushing my legs up towards my stomach and slammed inside me. I groaned, squeezing the sheet. He was thrusting inside me harder. He was increasing his pace thrust by thrust. I was moaning over and over.

My body trembled as I came, screaming his name out. A few thrusts later, he came inside me. He collapsed beside me. We were breathing heavily. He placed his hand on my cheek.

"How are you feeling?" He asked, panting.

"Wonderful." I murmured, grinning. He smirked at me and placed a tender kiss on my lips.

He got up and put on his sweatpants. I was laying on the bed. Tired and sore, looking at him. And probably, messy.

He looked at me and chuckled. "Get up, my little mess."

He extended his hand towards me, giving me an arrogant smirk. I smiled and held his hand. I got up and put his shirt on. I squeezed my lips together as I felt pain between my legs.

We headed to the kitchen. I was starving.

"Can you still sit?" He smirked at me, self-satisfied with himself.

I raised my eyebrow at him. "I missed your arrogance." I commented, sighing playfully. He laughed happily.

"Come on, eat something. Later, I will help with about your situation." He said, cupping my butt.

After having breakfast, we took a bath together. I felt better. The pain decreased.

I put on my clothes and went to the hotel.

Dimitri's POV

The elevator door opened; Nikolai walked in.

"Hey, my handsome playboy." He greeted playfully, smirking.

"Hey, man." I gave him a side hug.

"Do not say it. Someone can get you wrong. Everybody can not know that you are only jealous of my life." I warned him, smirking arrogantly.

"You got me. But I love my wife with her crazy pregnancy hormones." He stated, smirking. I laughed.

Nikolai was my childhood friend. We were close friends. He and his wife were university sweethearts. They got married six months ago. And they were expecting.

"Who can say you are the same womanizer now?!" I shook my head play-fully, smirking. He burst out laughing.

"I will see you, too." He winked at me, smirking.

"Whiskey?" I asked; he nodded.

I poured two glasses of whiskey for us. I handed him the glass while I was sipping my whiskey. I sat down on the couch.

"I saw Alyona today." He informed, sipping his whiskey.

"Hmm."

"You dumped her again?! She asked about you." He said.

"She has been getting on my nerves....Yes, she was good at pissing my father off. But I can not bear her anymore.... And I have another idea in my mind." I confessed, sipping my whiskey.

He shook his head with a disapproving expression.

"How much did pissing your father off cost you?" He asked.

"A little fortune." I replied, giving him a slight grin. He sighed.

"When will you forgive him?" He asked with a serious expression. I sighed.

"Nikolai, do not start again." I warned, annoyed.

I stood up and poured a glass of whiskey for myself.

"Ok, Dima." He said with an annoyed expression.

My phone buzzed. I took my phone. It was Sarah.

'Miss you.'

I grinned.

'Miss you, too, kiska.'

I sent a message to her and put my phone down.

"Is the reason of your stupid grin a woman with slender legs?" Nikolai asked, smirking arrogantly. I smirked at him.

"Not only with slender legs. With brown silky hair, mesmerizing brown eyes and a dazzling smile." I responded, grinning broadly.

Chapter 9 - Wifey for lifey

Dimitri's POV

He looked at me, surprised. "Wow! And who is that unlucky girl?" He asked, smirking. I laughed.

"I think she is lucky. So am I." I replied, giving him an arrogant smirk.

"Hmm." He raised his eyebrow with an amused expression on his face.

Sarah's POV

"Why are you sad?" Dimitri asked, placing his hand on top of my hand on the table.

We were having breakfast. My father and I were going back in two days.

"Because, I am going back in two days." I murmured sadly.

He looked at me tenderly, holding my hand.

"Do not be sad. And who knows? Maybe you will not go." He commented and winked at me.

I looked at him with inquiring eyes. "What do you mean?"

He shrugged his shoulder, giving me a knowing smile.

What is he planning?

I opened my eyes, stretching out. I got up and went to the bathroom.

After taking a shower, I put on a black tank top and navy blue shorts.

My father and I had breakfast. He said Uncle Sergei invited us for dinner tomorrow evening.

After having breakfast, my father went to Dimitri's company.

I was in my suite. Someone knocked on the door. I went towards the door and opened it.

"Ms. Miller, it is for you." The man handed me a big box.

"Umm... Thank you."

I took the box and closed the door. I went to my bedroom and placed the box on the bed. I opened it. There was a white lace dress in the box. I saw a note in the box.

'Today you are mine....Be ready. I will call you. Dimitri.'

I put on the dress. The dress was so beautiful and elegant. I did my hair wavy and left me hair open. I looked at myself in the mirror. My phone buzzed. I grabbed my phone.

'Waiting for you in front of the hotel.'

I smiled and put my phone into my clutch as I left.

I saw Dimitri in front of the hotel. He was leaning against his car. He wore a black suit, a white shirt and a black tie. He was extremely sexy.

I walked towards him. He smiled at me, wrapping his arm around my waist and kissed my lips.

"You are stunning, kiska." He murmured in my ear. "I look forward to taking your dress off." He added, kissing my neck. I blushed.

He pulled back and opened the door for me. I got in the car. He got in the car and started driving.

"Where are we going?" I asked in curiosity.

"You will see." He replied, smiling.

He held my hand and placed them together on his thigh as we entwined our hands. I smiled at him.

He parked his car. Dimitri got out of his car. He opened the door for me and extended his hand. I took his hand and got out of the car. He held my hand and headed us towards the church.

"What are we doing here, Dimitri?" I asked, confused.

He did not say anything.

He stopped in front of the church. He pulled something out from his pocket and got down on his one knee. I was surprised.

Is he going...?

I was speechless and totally nervous. He opened the box. There was a diamond ring in the box.

"Dimitri..." I murmured.

"Sarah, I know it seems crazy. It is not so long that we know each other. But I love you and want to spend my life with you. Will you marry me? Now and here."

I did not know what to say. He was looking into my eyes as he was waiting for my answer. It was so early. But my heart was saying the same word...Yes!

"I...Yes!" I replied, smiling. He smiled at me and slid the ring on my finger.

He stood up and hugged me tightly. I hugged him back.

Suddenly, we heard clapping. We pulled back. A man and a woman walked towards us, smiling.

"Sarah, let me introduce you to Nikolai, my best friend and his wife, Olga."

"Nice to meet you." I said, giving them a warm smile.

"I looked forward to meeting you. I wondered who was the girl who swept Dima off his feet." Nikolai confessed, smirking at Dimitri.

Dimitri furrowed his eyebrows at him. I smiled, holding his hand. He smiled at me, kissing my hair.

"You may now kiss the bride." The priest said.

Dimitri wrapped his arms around my waist, pulling me closer to him and brushed his lips against mine, kissing me softly. I wrapped my arms around his neck, kissing him back. He pulled back and leaned his forehead against mine.

We went to have dinner afterwards. Our reception dinner. It was the best day in my life. I was so happy. I am his wife. It was a crazy decision, but I didn't regret it.

Dimitri parked his car in front of his penthouse building. We got out of the car. He wrapped his arm around me, pulling me closer to him as he headed us towards the building.

The elevator door opened. He scooped me up in his arms bridal style.

"Welcome to our home, Mrs. Sarah Fedorova." He said, giving me a wide smile.

I smiled back, wrapping my arms around his neck and kissed his lips.

He carried me to the bedroom and set me down on my feet. There were red rose petals on the bed.

He cupped my cheek, looking into my eyes.

"Wifey for lifey." He commented with a mischievous smirk. I smiled.

He leaned closer and claimed my lips in a passionate kiss. I ran my hands through his hair. He was kissing me hungrily while he was unzipping my dress. I removed the straps of my dress, letting it slide down. He stepped back, roaming my body with salacious eyes.

"Stunning and mine."

He took off his jacket, tie and shirt without taking his eyes off me and threw them away, melting me with his intense gaze.

He cupped my cheek and kissed my lips hungrily, moving me back. We fell down onto the bed.

He was kissing me lustfully while he was moving his hand down my body. He pulled my lower lip between his teeth. I moaned, running my hands along his bare back. He slid his hand under my lace panties. I pursed my lips together in sensation. He pushed his finger inside me, making me moan. He added another finger, torturing me with his fingers while he was kissing my neck. I gripped his hair, moaning. He increased his pace. I arched my back and came, screaming his name out. He pulled his fingers out and put it into his mouth, looking into my eyes with full of passion in his eyes. He sucked his fingers, closing his eyes as he moaned.

He got up and took off his other clothes. He pulled my panties down and parted my legs apart wide, positioning himself between my legs. He slammed inside me roughly, making me moan louder.

"I...love.....you." He murmured between his thrusts.

Chapter 10 - The plan

Sarah's POV

It was dawn when we fell asleep. I was so tired.

I felt a soft hand on my hair, stroking my hair. I stretched out and opened my eyes. My eyes met a pair of beautiful green eyes. My husband's eyes. I smiled at him. He was only in his boxer, sitting beside me on the bed.

"Good morning." I said.

"Good morning, kiska." He greeted me, smiling at me. "Breakfast for my beautiful wife." He added, picking the tray up from the bedside table.

I sat up on the bed smiling, wrapping the cover around me.

"Thank you." I said happily.

After having breakfast, we took a shower together. A long shower. Thanks to my handsome husband who never gets tired.

Today we were going to tell our family about our marriage. I was so nervous. I called my father and said I was outside, and I was going to go to the mansion myself.

I put on my white dress; I didn't have my clothes here. Before dinner, Dimitri and I were going to my hotel to take my stuff, and I could change my clothes there.

I walked into the living room. Dimitri was here, waiting for me.

He smiled at me, wrapping his arm around me, pulling me closer to him.

"This dress reminds me of such mind-blowing memories." He confessed with a seductive voice, stroking my cheek.

I flushed, looking away. He smiled and held my hand.

We went to my hotel. I packed my suitcases and wore a black mini dress with sleeves.

Dimitri wrapped his arm around my waist from behind, pulling me closer to him. He pressed his bulge onto my back, trailing his lips along my neck.

"You look so sexy in this dress." He murmured in my ear seductively.

His breath fanned my neck, sending shivers down my spine. I felt a burning sensation between my legs. I was on fire. What is this man doing to me? I bit my lower lip.

He inhaled my scent. I closed my eyes, placing my hand on top of his hand on my stomach.

Suddenly, he pulled back, leaving me helpless and devastated. In need for his touches.

He smirked as he said huskily, looking at me with salacious eyes. "Let's go."

"Umm...Ok."

He took my suitcases as we left. We got in his car.

I was biting my lower lip, tapping my fingers on my thigh. He held my hand, placing our hands on his thighs.

"Do not worry." He gave me a reassuring smile. I nodded and smiled at him.

He parked his car in front of the mansion. He got out of the car. He opened the door for me and extended his hand towards me. I held his hand and got out of the car. He headed us towards the door, holding my hand.

He knocked on the door. The housekeeper opened the door. We walked in. I held his hand tightly. My heart was beating faster.

We walked into the living room. My father, Uncle Sergei, Valentina and a man, probably Valentina's husband were here.

"Good evening." Dimitri greeted them.

They were looking at us, surprised. Valentina saw my ring and smiled at us, surprised. My father was looking at me, shocked. Uncle Sergei looked at our hands, self-satisfied, giving us a knowing smile.

"Sarah, what is going on?" My father stood up as he asked angrily.

"Dad..."

"We got married yesterday." Dimitri confirmed, looking at them.

My father looked at me, then our hands and my ring, dumbfounded.

"Congratulations!" Valentina shouted happily and hugged us.

Later, his husband congratulated us. Uncle Sergei stood up and walked towards us. Dimitri was smirking at him arrogantly.

"Congratulations!" He exclaimed and hugged Dimitri.

Dimitri's face expression changed. He looked at him, shocked.

Then, his father hugged me. " Congratulations, my daughter-in-law." He stated, giving me a broad smile.

"Thank you." I said.

Dimitri was looking at his father angrily. He clenched his fist. His expression hardened.

What is going on?

"Sarah, we need to talk. Alone!" My father snapped, interrupting my thoughts. I looked at my father and nodded. We went to the garden.

Dimitri's POV

"Dimitri, come with me." My father ordered, smiling.

He walked towards the study room. I followed him. I walked into the study room and closed the door behind me. My father sat down on his seat, looking at me self-satisfied. I clenched my jaw.

Why is he so happy?

"Sit down!" He ordered, pointing to the seat.

"Why are you happy?" I asked coldly, putting my hands into my pockets, standing in front of him. I was frustrated. This was not what I had expected.

"Why should I not be happy? My son got married." He said calmly.

I breathed deeply, trying to calm down.

"You know damn well what I am talking about." I hissed, running my hand through my hair angrily.

He gave me an arrogant smile. "Why are you angry, Dimitri? Because your plan did not work?" He asked arrogantly.

I looked at him angrily. He shook his head, smirking.

"Do not forget, you are my son!" He reminded.

"Unfortunately!" I snapped, looking into his eyes. He sighed.

"When will you forgive me?" He asked sadly.

I laughed with a mocking smile. "Never." I replied. He sighed, looking upset.

"Do not be so sure, son! You do not know everything."

I breathed deeply. "Enough!" I snapped.

"I planned it. I wanted you to be together with Sarah. I know her; she is a caring, kind and beautiful girl. If I told you that she was the same girl who I wanted to introduce you, you wouldn't accept it. Because of me." He shook his head as he continued. "For that, I told you that I wanted you to marry my friend's daughter, Anastasia. And of course, you refused. At the restaurant, I saw how you looked at Sarah. Because of that, I told you to stay away from her. I knew you wouldn't listen to me. And you did not. But I should accept, I did not expect this so early." He entwined his hands on the desk, self-satisfied.

Damn it! Damn it!

I clenched my fist.

" Your plan blew up in your face?!" He commented arrogantly, shaking his head.

Chapter 11 - Not so perfect

- -

S arah's POV

My father and I were in the garden. I folded my arms over my chest nervously.

"Do you love him this much?" He asked me, trying to calm down.

I nodded, biting my lower lip. He sighed, shaking his head.

"I love him so much, Dad. I am sorry. I should tell you, but..." I gave him an apologetic look.

"I can not say I am so happy about it. Yes, he is a good guy. But I heard about his nightlife. And I am worried about you." He breathed deeply as he continued. "But.... if you are happy with him, it is enough for me. And do not forget I am by your side." He stated, giving me a tender smile.

"I love you, Dad." I confessed happily, hugging him. I was so relieved.

"I think, tomorrow I am going back alone." He commented in amusement. I smiled at him.

"I will miss you, my mother and brother."

"Be happy, dear. And if he will do something wrong to you, tell me. I will make him regret it." He said with a serious expression. I smiled as I nodded.

We went back to the living room. Dimitri and his father were not here. Valentina told me they were talking in the study room.

My father and Valentina's husband were talking in the garden. Valentina and I were in the living room.

"How far along are you pregnant?" Valentina asked me in a low voice. I looked at her, puzzled.

"I am not." I replied, blushing. She looked at me, surprised.

"Sorry. I thought you were. You got married so early because of that, I thought you were. And of course, I did not wait for Dimitri to marry so quickly." She commented, giving me an amused smile. I gave her a slight smile.

Suddenly, we heard a loud noise. Someone slammed the door.

Dimitri walked into the living room. He looked frustrated.

"We are going." He snapped at me, grabbing my wrist.

"What happened, Dima?" Valentina asked, worried.

Dimitri did not say anything. He walked out in quick steps, dragging me out with him. He was holding my wrist tightly. It was hurting.

"Dimitri, what happened?"

He did not answer me. He opened the door for me. I got in the car. He slammed the door, making me jolt. He got in the car and started driving.

He was driving too fast.

Why is he frustrated? Doesn't his father approve of our marriage? But he looked so happy.

"Dimitri! You are driving too fast." I warned, scared.

He gave me a mocking smirk.

"Does your father not approve of our marriage?" I asked, looking at him.

He clenched his jaw.

"No, he is too happy." He murmured mockingly.

What this means?

He stopped the car. We got out of the car. As soon as we walked into the penthouse, he poured whiskey into a glass and drank it in one sip. Then he took his jacket and tie off.

I walked towards him. He poured himself a glass of whiskey again. I placed my hand on his arm.

"Dimitri, tell me. What happened? You are not looking fine." I said, concerned.

He was sipping his whiskey without looking at me. He moved away and sat down on the couch, running his hand through his hair.

"Go to bed, Sarah." He ordered dryly without looking at me.

I walked towards him and sat down beside him. I held his hand.

"I will not leave you alone. You don't look fine." I said softly. He pulled his hand away.

"Sarah, go to bed." He hissed, emphasizing each word.

"Di..."

"Leave me the fuck alone!" He barked at me without letting me finish my sentence.

I looked at him, shocked. I had not seen him like this before. He was so angry. He ran his hand through his hair angrily.

I went to the bedroom. Insisting would not be good now. He was too angry. I changed my clothes and lay down on the bed.

I couldn't sleep. I was tossing and turning.

The sun was shining through the large windows.

I rubbed my eyes. I was so tired. I couldn't sleep properly last night.

When I looked at the other side of the bed, Dimitri was not here; he did not even sleep here last night.

I got up and put my silk robe on. I walked to the living room.

I saw him sleeping on the couch. There were empty bottles on the centre table. I walked closer to him and sat down on the centre table. I looked at him.

"What is bothering you?" I asked, stroking his blond hair.

I sighed and stood up. I kissed his lips and went to the kitchen.

I was making pancakes in the kitchen, lost in my thoughts.

When I turned around, I saw Dimitri. He was looking at me with a blank expression.

"Good morning. How are you feeling?" I asked, looking at him.

"Morning. Fine." He mumbled and walked towards the fridge. He poured himself a glass of cold water. He opened the drawer and pulled something out. He took a painkiller.

"Breakfast is ready. I made pancakes." I informed softly, looking at him.

He looked at me with a blank expression.

"I am not hungry. I am going. And I have a housekeeper. You do not need to make breakfast." He stated coldly and left the kitchen without letting me say anything.

I did not understand what had happened to him.

Why is he distant and cold towards me?

I sighed, depressed.

A few minutes later, I heard the elevator door open and close.

"Dimitri?" I called him, but he had already left; he left without saying goodbye. I felt pain. I sat down, looking into space.

"Good morning. You must be Mrs. Fedorova. Nice to meet you. I am Galina, the housekeeper." A middle-aged woman interrupted me from my thoughts.

"Umm...Good morning. Nice to meet you, too. Call me Sarah." I said.

She gave me a polite smile and nodded.

"Are you fine?" She asked, concerned.

I nodded and stood up. She looked at the table, our untouchable breakfast, but she did not say anything.

I went to the bedroom. I took a shower and put on a beige blouse and black shorts. I did not feel well. I was lying on the bed.

Suddenly, my phone buzzed. I took my phone, excited. It was Dimitri. I opened the message, excited.

'Don't wait for me for dinner. I will be late.'

I read the message again and again. My eyes flooded with tears. I placed my phone down on the bed and wrapped my arms around my legs.

Chapter 12 - Heartbreak

S arah's POV

It was midnight, but Dimitri had not come back yet. I was waiting for him in the living room. I called him, but his phone was turned off.

Where are you? And with whom?

I woke up to noises. I had fallen asleep on the couch while waiting for him. I stood up immediately.

It was Dimitri. He was drunk. He was barely standing on his feet.

"Dimitri!" I walked towards him. He gave me an arrogant grin.

"Kiska..." He murmured, giving me a half smile.

I held his arm to help him, but he pulled his arm away as he walked to the bedroom, placing his hand on the wall for support. I followed him.

He collapsed onto the bed, unbuttoning his shirt.

"Where have you been?" I asked.

It was enough, he should give me an explanation.

What is wrong with him?

He arched his eyebrows, looking at me bemused.

"Kiska...kiska...do you know how sexy you look when you are angry?" He asked, looking at me lustfully.

"Dimitri, stop it! What is wrong with you? Tell me! Now!" I demanded angrily, putting my hands on my hips.

He gave me a sarcastic smirk.

"You do not really know?! I hate you! I hate my father!" He hissed, looking into my eyes with full of anger in his eyes.

What?

I hate you. This sentence repeated in my mind. I felt heartbroken.

"Why?" I asked. My voice was barely audible.

I was holding my tears back hard. He looked at me sarcastically.

"Do not fool me! My father has planned it, and you helped him." He snarled.

"What are you talking about? What plan?" I asked. I did not understand what he was talking about.

"Our wedding. He said he wanted me to marry you. Because of that, he told me to stay away from you. Because he knew if he told me, I wouldn't do it. But he did not wait for it to happen so early. And I need to thank you, you were good at acting."

His every word made me feel worse. He married me, because he wanted to piss his father off.

What a fool I was!

"You married me for it?" I murmured, holding my tears back. He looked at me, puzzled. "You married me to piss your father off?" I shouted at him. His expression softened.

"You did not know about my father's plan?" He asked, surprised.

"Of course not. Do you think I am crazy to get married to anyone...who doesn't love me?" I snapped at him.

"I did not say that I did not love you." He said, looking into my eyes. I sighed, closing my eyes.

"We do not say I hate you when we love this person." I commented, giving him a fake smile.

"Sorry.... I thought you knew the plan."

I shook my head, looking at him, offended. He was not the man who I loved.

He grabbed my wrist.

"Do not touch me!" I snapped, pulling my hand away, sobbing.

He did not let me, pulling me into his lap, hugging me tightly, burying his head into my hair. I was punching his chest, sobbing. He was stroking my hair.

"Sorry. Sorry." He repeated.

"And you decided to make me pay. Fucking someone else while I was waiting for you while I was worried about you." I hissed, sobbing. He held my head in his hands.

"Never. I will never cheat on you. I will not do like him. Never. You are the only woman who I want to touch. Only you." He stated with a serious expression.

He brushed his lips against mine, kissing me passionately, pulling me closer to him. He tried to shove his tongue into my mouth, but I did not let him. He bit my lower lip slightly and plunged his tongue into my mouth, exploring my mouth with his professional tongue.

After a while, I responded to his demanding kiss, moving my hands along his bare chest.

He pulled me closer to him, pressing me against his hard bulge. I moaned. He took my blouse off and threw it away, kissing my neck. He unclasped my bra. He moved his lips down to my breast, cupping, kissing them, making me moan louder. I gripped his hair, squeezing my eyes shut.

I slid my hands under his shirt and removed it. He placed me on the bed, kissing me hungrily. He slid his hand under my panties, cupping me between my legs. I gasped in desire. His every touch made me lose control more and more.

A few seconds later, we were naked. He parted my legs apart wide, positioning himself between my legs. He kissed my neck and slammed inside me without warning. I groaned, gripping his shoulders. He started thrusting inside me harder and deeper, making me moan louder.

He hit my sensitive spot. I came, screaming his name out. He reclaimed my lips, thrusting inside me.

"I love you." He murmured, coming inside me.

He rolled over, trying to catch his breath. He pulled me into his embrace. I placed my head on his chest, closing my eyes.

I opened my eyes, stretching out. Dimitri was not in the bed. The room was messy. The messy sheet and our clothes scattered all over the floor.

I looked at the watch on the bedside table. It was 11:00 a.m.

Where is Dimitri?

I noticed a note on the bedside table. I got up and took it.

'I am going to New York for a week. I have a meeting there. I will call you. See you later.

Dimitri.'

My tears were dripping on the note. I crumbled the note and threw it away onto the floor.

He regretted what happened last night. He did not even wake me up. I hated myself. I felt cheap.

Stupid, Sarah!

He fucked you and ran away without saying goodbye like you were a slut.

I walked into the bathroom, placing my hand on the wall for support. I felt dizzy. My legs were trembling. I turned on warm water. The droplets were dripping down, mixing with my tears.

Chapter 13 - Torture

Sarah's POV

When I went to the living room, Galina was here.

"Good morning, Sarah. Breakfast is ready." Galina said, giving me a smile.

"Good morning. Thanks, but I am not hungry." I mumbled. I did not want to eat anything.

"Are you feeling fine?" She asked, concerned. I nodded. She gave me an unconvinced look, but she did not insist.

I was watching the sky through the window. I felt weak and sad.

My phone rang. This was my mother. I picked up my phone.

"Hi, Mom."

"Hi, Sarah. Your father told me about your marriage..."

"Mom, I am sorry...It happened so fast." I said, trying to control my voice.

"Too fast, dear. Too fast. I don't even know him. At least, your father and brother met him." She commented, offended.

"I am sorry, Mom." I murmured.

"Sarah....are you pregnant?"

"No, Mom. I am not pregnant." I replied.

Why does everyone ask the same question?

Of course, they would ask. Just you were a hopeless romantic. Getting married to the man who you had known for two weeks. The man who had left you in his country alone three days after your wedding. I shook my head.

"Mom, I need to go. I will call you later." I mumbled as my eyes filled with tears.

"Ok, Sarah. Bye."

I hung up, crying.

Three weeks later.

Dimitri's POV

"How is the weather in St. Petersburg?" Nikolai asked, smirking. I looked at him with questioning eyes.

"What are you talking about, Nikolai?!"

We were in my penthouse in New York. Nikolai had a meeting here. I finished my work in New York, but I couldn't go back like something was holding me back.

"Your body is here, but your mind and soul are in St. Petersburg." He commented, giving me a knowing smile. "Why are you here? You don't have a meeting or anything to do here. And you miss her. You call Galina every day and ask about her like a creepy husband. Do not be so stubborn.

Go to her. You should be there making love, spending passionate nights with your wife instead of being here." He added.

I was looking into space, thinking. I really missed her so much. Her smile, her silky hair, her touches. Galina told me she was not fine. I was worried about her, but I didn't have courage to call her. Because I knew if I would hear her voice, I couldn't stay away from her.

A few hours later, Nikolai left. I was sipping my whiskey while looking out. It was raining. The weather was gloomy like my mood.

My phone rang. I placed my glass on the centre table and took my phone. It was Galina. I picked up the phone.

"Hi, Galina. How is Sarah today?" I asked anxiously. I was worried.

She sighed without saying anything.

"What happened, Galina? Is she okay?" I asked, worried.

"Dimitri, she is not fine. She doesn't eat anything or leave her room. Today, I insisted on her having breakfast. After eating a little, she vomited. I told her that I would call the doctor, but she didn't let me. You should come back, Dimitri. She needs you."

I clenched my fist. "Ok, Galina. I am coming."

I hung up my phone and rushed to my bedroom. I packed my suitcase and left as soon as possible.

Sarah's POV

I was laying on the bed. I felt weak and numb. I stayed at home without leaving the penthouse for a second. I did not have energy for getting up or eating.

Dimitri was still in New York. He had called me once since he went to New York. Later, I had called him a few times, but he did not pick up his phone.

I heard a knock on the door.

"Come in." I said barely.

Galina walked in, holding a tray in her hands.

"Good morning. How are you today?"

"Good morning. Fine." I murmured. She sighed, unconvinced.

"Come on, eat something." She suggested.

"I do not want to." I murmured, pulling the cover up a little.

"You should eat. You will get sick. Please." She said, concerned.

"Ok." I murmured and sat up.

She placed the tray on my lap. I started eating.

Suddenly, I felt nauseated. I placed the tray on the bed and rushed to the bathroom, covering my mouth with my hand. I had been feeling sick and dizzy the last few weeks. I couldn't eat properly.

After throwing up, I washed my face. I looked at myself in the mirror. My face was pale. I went back to the bedroom.

"How are you feeling?" She asked, concerned.

"Bad." I murmured, placing my hand on my stomach. My nausea had not passed yet.

I sat down on the bed. Galina walked towards me, placing her hand on my shoulder.

"Let me call the doctor."

"No! I do not want to. I want to sleep." I stated and lay down on the bed, pulling the cover over my body.

She sighed and took the tray. She walked out, closing the door behind her.

I did not feel well again, I wanted to vomit. I got up and put on my silk robe.

When I was going to the bathroom, I felt dizzy. I placed my hand on the wall for support. My vision darkened.

Dimitri's POV

Finally, the jet landed in St. Petersburg. I called Galina as soon as I got off the jet. She said Sarah was sleeping. I got in my car and went home. I was driving fast.

I parked my car in front of my penthouse building. I got out of the car. I walked into my penthouse in quick steps.

"Welcome, Dimitri." Galina greeted me.

"Where is Sarah?" I asked.

"She is in the bedroom."

I went to the bedroom. I knocked on the door and walked in. I froze in my place when I saw Sarah laying on the floor with her eyes closed. Her face was pale.

"Sarah!" I shouted, frightened.

Chapter 14 - The difficult decision

Dimitri's POV

I rushed towards her.

"Sarah." I stroked her hair.

I scooped her up in my arms and carried her to the bed. I put her on the bed carefully.

"Sarah?! What happened?" Galina walked in as she asked, looking at her in worry.

"Call the doctor." I shouted, frightened. She nodded and walked out.

I sat beside Sarah on the bed, stroking her hair, cheek.

She lost weight. Her face was pale. I was angry at myself. It was my fault.

A few minutes later, she opened her eyes slowly. She looked at me, surprised and puzzled .

"How are you feeling? The doctor is coming." I asked, holding her hand.

She was looking at me coldly without saying anything. She sat up, pulling her hand away.

"What are you doing here?" She murmured without looking at me.

"It is my home too, kiska." I replied amusingly, looking at her. I was holding myself hard not to hug her. I missed her so much. "I was worrying about you." I added.

"I am fine." She murmured.

I placed my hand on top of her hand.

"I am sorry, Sarah." I confessed, giving her an apologetic look. She did not say anything.

Finally, the doctor came. I stood up.

"Hello, Mr. Fedorov."

I shook her hand. "Hello, Mrs. Borisova. She fainted." I informed. She nodded.

"Hello, Mrs. Fedorova. I am Polina Borisova." She said, looking at Sarah.

"Hello. I am Sarah." She said, giving her a slight smile.

"Mr. Fedorov, could you wait outside?" She asked.

I nodded, looking at Sarah and walked out, closing the door behind me.

Sarah's POV

Dimitri was here. Firstly, I thought I was dreaming. But he was really here. Telling me he missed me like nothing had happened.

He left the room, leaving me with the doctor alone. The doctor gave me a smile and sat down beside me. She checked my blood pressure.

"Your blood pressure is low. When have you eaten the last time?"

I pursed my lips together, playing with the cover.

"I couldn't. I felt nauseated." I admitted. She smiled at me.

"Are you late?" She asked.

I looked at her, dumbfounded. I was late. I couldn't think straight anymore.

No! No!

It was not the right time.

Please no!

She opened her bag and pulled a box out of it. She gave me a warm smile and handed me the box. I took it with my trembling hand.

"Do a test." She said.

I got up and went to the bathroom, grabbing the box tightly.

I did the test and walked out, holding the test. I did not want a baby now, especially in these terms. My hands were cold.

The doctor took the test and looked at it.

"You are pregnant. Congratulations." She stated, smiling.

I couldn't breathe anymore.

Fuck! Pregnant. Pregnant.

"Are you feeling fine? Your face is pale." She asked.

Fine? Why shouldn't I?!

I was pregnant by the man who did not love me, and even he moved away not to see my face.

"Yes...I am." I murmured. My voice was barely audible.

"You should make an appointment with an obstetrician." She informed.

I nodded. She stood up and took her bag.

"Umm...please, do not tell Dimitri....I want to tell him myself." I lied.

I needed some time. She nodded, unconvinced and walked out.

Dimitri's POV

I was sitting in front of the door, leaning against the wall, waiting for the doctor. I was worrying about Sarah.

Finally, the doctor walked out. I stood up quickly.

"How is she?" I asked anxiously. She gave me a smile.

"Do not worry, Mr. Fedorov. She is fine. Her blood pressure was low. She is fine now." She informed.

I breathed deeply, running my hand through my hair. I was relieved.

"Thank you."

She nodded and walked away. I walked into the bedroom.

Sarah was laying on the bed. I walked towards her and sat down beside her on the bed. I placed my hand on top of her hand. She did not look at me and pulled her hand away.

"I am sorry, Sarah. I am damn sorry."

She did not say anything. I sighed.

"You need to rest." I commented and stood up.

I will do everything for your forgiveness. I promise. I said with my inner voice.

Sarah's POV

A few minutes later, Dimitri came back, holding a tray in his hands.

"You should eat." He said and sat down beside me. I nodded.

He placed the tray on his lap. There was some soup in the bowl. He extended the spoon towards me.

"I can eat myself." I stated coldly, trying to grab the spoon.

"Sarah, please...let me." He begged, giving me puppy eyes. I sighed and opened my mouth.

The soup was so delicious. I was so hungry.

I finished eating.

"Thank you." I murmured.

He gave me his charming smile. He placed the tray on the bedside table.

"Sarah....I..."

I interrupted him. "I want to sleep. I am tired."

He nodded and stood up. "Ok, we will talk later."

He leaned towards me and placed a soft kiss on my forehead. I closed my eyes. My nostrils filled with his smell. The same smell, which drove me crazy.

No, Sarah! He doesn't deserve you....And us.

He took the tray and walked out, closing the door behind him. I leaned back against the pillow, placing my hand on my stomach.

"My baby." I rubbed my stomach.

My eyes filled with tears. I needed to decide. The most difficult decision in my life. I lay down, pulling my legs towards my chest, wrapping my arms around my stomach.

When I woke up, it was noon. I took my iPad and found the obstetrician. I grabbed my phone and called.

"Hello. I want to make an appointment with Mrs. Ivanova for tomorrow." I informed.

"Hello, Ma'am. Ok, I will check. Please, wait a minute....tomorrow...at 10.00 a.m."

"Yes. It is okay."

"Your name and surname?"

"Sarah Fedorova."

"Check up...."

"An abortion." I muttered.

"Ok."

I hung up, placing the phone down. I placed my hand on my stomach, rubbing it.

"I am so sorry. But I can not. I am sorry." I muttered, crying.

Chapter 15 - Be my breath

I got up and went to the bathroom. Dimitri did not sleep here last night.

After taking a shower, I put on my clothes and took my bag.

Dimitri was not in the penthouse. Galina said he had left early, but he would come back at noon. I told Galina that I was going to meet up with my friend.

I was waiting for the doctor. I was so nervous. The nurse called me. I walked into the room, gripping the strap of my bag tightly.

"Hello, Mrs. Fedorova. My name is Luba." The doctor greeted me. "Sit down, please." She pointed to the chair, giving me a slight smile.

I sat down, biting my lower lip nervously.

"Well...I need to ask. Are you sure?" She asked.

Am I? No, but I should do it.

"Yes." I muttered. My voice was barely audible.

"Ok, but firstly, let's check up. Lie down and pull your blouse up." She said. I nodded and stood up.

She put the gel on my stomach. My heart was beating faster.

"You are about six weeks pregnant." She informed.

I couldn't look at the screen. Suddenly, the room filled with heartbeats.

"These are..." I murmured, looking at the doctor, holding my tears back hardly. She nodded.

"Yes, it is your baby's heartbeats." She confirmed.

I was so emotional. I couldn't hold my tears anymore. I looked at the screen.

My little bean.

The doctor handed me some tissues as she stood up. I wiped the gel off my stomach and got up.

"Are you sure? Do you want to get an abortion?" She asked me.

My baby's heartbeats were still repeating in my mind. But I should do it.

"...I...Yes." I muttered. She nodded.

"Ok, the nurse will help you to get ready." She informed and called the nurse, leaving me alone in the room.

I placed my hand on my stomach. "I am sorry, my little bean." I said, sobbing.

My phone rang. I pulled my phone out of my bag. It was Dimitri. I switched the volume to mute.

The nurse walked in. "Mrs. Fedorova, take your clothes off and put on it."

I started unbuttoning my blouse slowly. My hands were shaking.

"No. No. I can not do it." I said, buttoning my blouse up quickly.

The doctor walked in.

"I can not do it. I can not." I confessed, looking at her. She gave me a smile, nodding.

"Ok. Then, let me give you some information about pregnancy." She said. I nodded, smiling.

Then I left the hospital. I was so happy. It was the right decision. I couldn't do it to my little bean. I couldn't kill her or him. I was going to be a mother.

My little bean.

I rubbed my stomach.

When I arrived, Dimitri was not in the penthouse. Galina told me he called a few times; he was worrying about me. She told me he was on the way. I nodded and went to my room.

I started packing my suitcases. I couldn't stay here anymore. I decided to go back to New York, but before I needed to be alone. I went to the living room, pulling my suitcase with me.

"Sarah, where have you been?..." Dimitri asked as he walked in. He didn't finish his sentence when he saw my suitcase. He looked at me with the mixture of fear and shock in his eyes.

"You..." He murmured, looking into my eyes.

"I am going." I informed.

"Where?" He muttered barely.

"I do not know. I need to be alone." I replied, looking at him.

"No. No. Do not leave me! Please, don't leave me!" He begged, looking frightened.

"Dimitri..."

"No, do not leave me. I am begging you. Do not leave me!" He pleaded and knelt down on his knees in front of me. I was shocked.

"Dimitri...stand up...please...." I muttered. He shook his head.

"Please, Sarah...do not leave me. I love you so much. I can not bear it...this time. Do not leave me!" He said, sobbing.

I walked towards him and knelt down beside him. I had not seen him like this.

This time? What is going on?

I remembered the night when he was drunk. 'I will not do like him.' There was something.

"What are you talking about, Dimitri? I do not understand. What is the problem between you and your father? And you... you do not love me. Even you had left me. Why? Why do you want me to stay?"

He looked at me, wiping his tears off his cheeks.

"My mother had left my sister and me when I was five years old. Because of my father. I have not seen her after that day. I had heard their fight. They were fighting, yelling at each other. She mentioned a woman, something about it. The next day, she left." He sighed and continued. "For that, I hate my father. I did everything to make him angry. All my girlfriends were someone who he wouldn't approve of. All of these were for making him angry. " He paused as he looked into my eyes. "Later, I met you. I really like you at first sight. You were so beautiful. And you are as always. My father told me that he wanted me to marry his friend's daughter, some Russian businessman's daughter, and he told me to stay away from you." He breathed deeply and continued. "And then, I decided to make you my girlfriend. But it was not just for my father. I really wanted it too...So much. When your leaving date came closer, I decided to propose. I did not want to lose you. You are the only woman who I want in my life. You are my breath. And my father's disapproval was a bonus. But when we told them about our marriage, he told me he had planned it. He told me to stay away from you purposely, because he knew I wouldn't obey him. I thought you were in it too, but later, when we talked, you told me you did not know anything. But I was angry at my father...at you. I know it is not your fault....but...." He shrugged his shoulders.

I was shocked. I did not know what to say. I was speechless.

My poor boy.

"I love you, Sarah. I really love you. I have been thinking about you all time when I was in New York. I couldn't call you because I knew if I would hear your voice, nothing could hold me back there...even my anger. I love you. Please, forgive me. I am so sorry. I promise I will not break your heart again. I will do everything to make you happy. Be my breath." He looked at me with begging eyes.

All my anger was gone. I hugged him, crying. He wrapped his arms around me, hugging me tightly, kissing my cheeks, forehead and hair.

"I love you. I love you." He repeated, kissing me.

"I love you too, Dimitri." I said and kissed his lips.

Our soft kiss turned into a passionate one. He helped me to stand up without separating our lips.

In a swift movement, he lifted me up. I wrapped my legs around his waist, running my hands through his hair. He carried me to the bedroom, kissing me hungrily.

Chapter 16 - The truth

S arah's POV

When I woke up, Dimitri was not in bed.

No. No. Don't do it to me again. I repeated with my inner voice.

Suddenly, the door opened. Dimitri walked in, holding the tray in his hands, smiling at me.

"Good morning, kiska."

"Good morning." I said, giving him a bright smile.

He walked closer to me and sat down beside me on the bed, placing the tray on the bed.

"Thank you, my romantic husband." I said and kissed his lips.

"You are welcome."

We started eating.

Suddenly, his phone rang. When he looked at his phone, he furrowed his eyebrows as he picked up his phone.

"Good morning, Dad."

He was listening to him, his eyebrows furrowed.

"Ok." He sighed and hung up his phone.

"I have to go to the company." He informed, giving me an apologetic look. I nodded.

"What about dinner?" He asked, caressing my hand.

"Great!" I exclaimed, smiling.

"Ok, I will pick you up. See you later." He said and kissed my lips.

I was watching him while he was putting on his clothes. He wore a black suit, a white shirt and a black tie. He placed a soft kiss on my lips and left.

Dimitri's POV

My father's voice was angry. He snapped at me and hung up.

I got out of my car and went to his office. I knocked on the door and walked in.

"Dad."

He looked frustrated.

"Sit down. We have to talk. I am not going to watch how you are messing up with your life." He snapped, looking at me angrily. I clenched my jaw.

"Dad..." I hissed.

"Do not interrupt me. You need to know the truth. Maybe then, you will stop acting like this."

I looked at him with questioning eyes.

What is he talking about?

"The truth?" I asked.

"About your mother."

I clenched my fist. "What are you talking about?" I hissed.

"Your mother has left us not because of that I cheated. She had left with her lover."

I looked at him, shocked. I shook my head as I laughed mockingly.

"Now you start lying about her. How pathetic!" I hissed.

"It is the truth. Your sister knows about it too. If you do not believe me, you can ask her. I had found out about it a week before she left. We fought and she accepted. She said she loved him and decided to go with him. I was frustrated and felt betrayed."

I was shocked. I felt like my world fell apart.

How? How?

I could not think straight anymore. My father was explaining, but I could not believe my ears.

"Why did you not tell me?" I murmured. My voice was barely audible.

"You loved your mother so much. There was a strong bond between you. I did not want to break your heart. But now, I am not going to watch how you ruin your life." He stated and looked at me softly. "Sarah loves you. You love her too. Do not ruin your life, your marriage for a lie." He added.

I ran my hand through my hair. All of those were for a lie. For a fucking lie. I clenched my fist. I looked at my father.

"I am sorry, Dad. I..."

"I understand you, son." He interrupted me.

"I hired a detective to find her. He found her, but she disappeared before I went to her house. I thought it was you who blackmailed her to stay away from us. I am really sorry, Dad." I said, giving him an apologetic look.

He stood up and walked towards me. I stood up. He hugged me. I hugged him back.

"I love you, son. You are my own flesh and blood. How can I be angry at you?! You will understand when you become a father." He stated, hugging me.

Sarah's POV

I went to the bathroom and took a shower. After drying myself with a towel, I put on my clothes and went to the kitchen. I had breakfast.

I wanted to buy a new dress for dinner. I took my bag and left.

I bought a black lace mini dress. It was so beautiful and sexy.

I stopped in front of the baby clothes shop. A pair of white shoes caught my attention. They were so cute. I smiled, placing my hand on my stomach, rubbing my belly. I walked into the shop. I decided to make Dimitri a surprise. After buying the shoes, I went to the penthouse.

It was evening. Dimitri was on the way. I got ready. I put the little box into my bag. My phone buzzed.

'I am waiting for you in front of the penthouse.'

I took my phone and left.

Dimitri was leaning against his car, waiting for me. He smiled at me as he saw me and looked at me from head to toe. I smiled at him back. He approached me and wrapped his arm around my waist, pulling me into his embrace.

"Stunning." He commented, looking into my eyes with pure passion in his eyes.

He placed a soft kiss on my lips. He held my hand, leading us to the car.

We were eating our dinner, listening to beautiful music. Dimitri stood up and walked towards me.

"Dance with me." He said, looking into my eyes as he extended his hand towards me. I smiled and gave my hand.

He wrapped his arms around my waist, pulling me closer to him, inhaling my hair. I wrapped my arms around his neck, leaning my head against his chest. Time seemed to stop. I was in heaven. In my heaven.

After having dinner, we went home. He held my hand, leading us to our bedroom. He sat down on the bed, looking at me with salacious eyes. He wrapped his arms around my waist, looking into my eyes. I stroked his hair.

"I need to tell you something." I informed.

He looked at me with questioning eyes. I took my bag and pulled the box out of my bag. I was so excited. I bit my lower lip nervously and handed him the box. He took the box, looking at me with a curious look. He untied the white ribbon slowly. My heart was beating faster. He opened the box. He took the shoes, looking into my eyes, opening and closing his mouth.

"You..." He said with inquiring eyes.

"I am pregnant." I informed happily.

Chapter 17 - The past

"I am going to be a father?!" He stated, looking at the shoes.

He lifted his head up and looked into my eyes. The spark of joy appeared in his eyes. He placed the shoes on the bed and stood up. He wrapped his arms around my waist and spun me around.

"I am going to be a father." He repeated happily.

I wrapped my arms around his neck, laughing happily. He set me down on my feet and cupped my cheeks.

"I love you." He confessed and brushed his lips against mine.

He pulled back, leaning his forehead against mine.

"I love you too." I said.

He placed his hand on my stomach and stroked it gently. He pulled back a little and kissed my lips passionately. I wrapped my arms around his neck, running my fingers through his hair. He started unzipping my dress. He moved his lips down to my neck, removing my dress.

We were laying on the bed. He placed his head on my stomach, caressing it gently. I was stroking his hair. I felt so happy.

****

When I woke up, Dimitri was telling our son a fairy tale, caressing my baby bump. Time flew so quickly; I was eight months pregnant now. We were going to have a boy. After learning about my pregnancy, Dimitri told our son fairy tales every day. He was so caring, affectionate towards us.

I stroked his hair. "Good morning."

He lifted his head up and smiled at me. "Morning, kiska."

He put a tender kiss on my lips.

"Let's have lunch together today." He suggested, stroking my cheek with his thumb. I nodded in agreement.

"Great. The driver will fetch you to the company. There is a new Italian restaurant near the company. Their food is delicious. You should try."

"Ok. I can't wait." I admitted, caressing my bump.

I arrived at the company and went to his room. I knocked on his door and walked in.

When he saw me, he stood up, smiling.

"Hey." I smiled at him.

He wrapped his arm around my waist and kissed my lips.

"I missed you" He said as he pulled his lips away.

"So do I." I admitted as I caressed his cheek.

"Hey, buddy, what are you doing here?" He said, grinning while stroking my bump.

"Kicking his mother." I replied, grinning. He smiled, placing a soft kiss on my stomach.

"I will grab my phone, and we can leave." He said. I nodded.

He went towards his desk and grabbed his phone.

"Let's go." He held my hand as we walked out.

Suddenly, he stopped as we saw a woman in the hallway. He clenched his jaw as he was squeezing my hand tightly.

"Sir..." His secretary wanted to say something, but she stopped under his intimidating gaze.

"Dimitri." The woman walked closer to us, looking at him sadly.

She was about in her late forties, but she looked younger than her age; she was beautiful and feminine in her black elegant wrap dress.

"Mom?" Dimitri mumbled; it was barely audible.

Of course, it was her.

She looked like him, especially with her green eyes in the same shades of green like Dimitri and Valentina's eyes.

He tightened his grip; it hurt my hand.

"Dimitri, you are hurting me." I whispered, trying to pull my hand.

He looked at my hand, dumbfounded, unaware of his tight grip. Then he released my hand.

"We need to talk." The woman stated.

Dimitri sighed deeply and looked at me as he said. "Sarah, give me a minute, please." He traveled his eyes from me to her. "It will not take long." He added bitterly.

I nodded. He walked into his office without waiting for her. She gave me a slight smile and followed him.

Dimitri's POV

She was here. Standing in front of me like nothing has happened. After all these years. What does she want? Why did she come back?

All these questions were repeating in my mind. I sat down on my seat. She walked in, closing the door behind her.

"What do you want? I don't have so much time." I stated dryly.

"I wanted to see you. I missed you, Dimitri." She said, giving me a warm smile. That smile which remembered me about my happy childhood.

I shook my head like I wanted to get rid of these thoughts. I looked at her as I said mockingly. "Really?!"

Is she thinking that after all these years when she comes back, I will hug her and say that I missed her?

She gave me a sad smile.

"Dimitri...."

"What do you want?" I interrupted her as I asked, emphasizing each word.

When she wanted to come closer, I raised my hand as I demanded. "Don't!"

"Dimitri, please. I need to explain to you."

I laughed mockingly. "Don't you think you are late for fucking twenty years?!" I barked at her as I stood up.

"I am sorry." She said; her eyes filled with tears.

"For what?! Do you know how I felt after you had left? Let me tell you. I had screwed my life. I even put my marriage in danger for what....." I gave a disgusting look. "Out of reason. I searched for you. But you ran every time. I thought it was for my father who had threatened you, but...." I gave her a fake smile. "I was waiting for you every damn day. Now you came like nothing has happened." I shook my head. "Now go! I do not need you in my life anymore. I do not want to see you. Get out of here!" I barked at her.

"Dimitri..."

"Get out of here!" I shouted.

She left without saying anything.

I pushed everything off the desk, making it shattered across the floor.

Sarah's POV

I was waiting for him in the hall. I felt worried and nervous; he didn't look fine. I heard his voice through the door. As if our baby felt about all of these, he was moving actively and kicking me hard, making me hurt. I caressed my bump, trying to calm down.

Several minutes later, the door opened. The woman left his office, crying.

When she saw me, she walked closer to me, wiping her tears off her cheeks with the back of her hand.

"You must be Sarah." She said, giving me a slight smile.

I nodded as I stood up.

She looked at my belly, smiling.

"How far along are you?" She asked without taking her eyes off my stomach.

"Eight months." I replied, caressing my baby bump.

"Nice to meet you, Sarah." She said and left without waiting for my answer.

I watched her leave, but suddenly, I heard noises coming from Dimitri's office.

Chapter 18 - Bliss

Sarah's POV

I rushed to his office, worried. As soon as I walked in, I saw him sadly sitting on his seat, holding his head in his hands, looking down. There was the glass scattered on the floor.

"Dimitri." I approached him.

He lifted his head up, looking sadly. I hugged him. He stood up as he hugged me back tightly and buried his head into the hollow on my neck. I caressed his hair.

"Are you fine?" I asked as I pulled my head away a little. He nodded.

"Sarah...sorry...but I need to talk to my father." He said.

"No problem, darling." I placed a tender kiss on his lips.

"The driver will drop you off." He informed. I nodded in agreement.

It was late, but Dimitri hadn't still come home. I was looking through the window, drinking my orange juice.

Suddenly, I heard noises; I placed my glass on the table and went towards the door.

"Kiska." Dimitri said in a gloomy voice as he wrapped his arms around me.

I hugged him back.

"How do you feel?" I asked, concerned.

"Complicated." He sighed and held my hand, leading us towards the couch.

We sat down on the couch. I leaned against his chest. He wrapped his arm around me, placing a soft kiss on my hair. He placed his free hand on my stomach and rubbed it tenderly.

"It is really bliss holding you in my arms...after a tough day." He murmured, caressing my hair.

I lifted my head and kissed his cheek.

"I love you." I said.

He smiled at me and kissed my lips. "I love you, too." He stroked my hair and suggested. "Let's go to bed. I am tired."

I nodded. We stood up; he wrapped his arm around me as we headed towards our bedroom.

I woke up to the delicious smell. I rubbed my eyes as I looked at the bed; Dimitri wasn't in the bed. I got up and put on my silk black robe. I headed towards the kitchen, following the heavenly smell.

I found Dimitri cooking in the kitchen. I folded my arms over my chest, leaning against the door frame. His back was turned to me. So he didn't notice me. He wore a white shirt, black suit pants and a black tie. As he turned around, he saw me.

"Morning, kiska." He said happily.

"Good morning." I smiled as I approached him. I wrapped my arms around him. He kissed my lips.

"My morning is good now." He commented. I smiled.

He placed his hand on my stomach and rubbed my belly.

"Hey, buddy, good morning to you too. Dad cooked you delicious pancakes." He said, still rubbing my bump.

"Only for him?" I asked, narrowing my eyes at him playfully.

He laughed and kissed my lips.

"My boy, your mother is jealous." He commented and placed a kiss on my stomach.

I smiled as I stroked his hair. "How do you feel?" I asked, concerned.

His expression hardened. "I am fine. Don't worry. Come on, let's have breakfast." He charged subjects.

I nodded without insisting.

After having breakfast, we went to the hospital; we had a doctor appointment.

The doctor was checking our baby. Dimitri and I were looking at the screen while she was moving the wand on my stomach.

"Yes....everything is normal. Your baby is healthy. But you should be more careful. Don't tire yourself too much." She said.

I nodded. Dimitri helped me to get up.

We left the hospital and went shopping for our baby. There were a lot of cute clothes in the baby shop. I couldn't decide which clothes to choose; all of them were adorable. We ended up buying plenty of different clothes. Then, we bought a lot of toys. His nursery room was ready. We decorated it in white, navy blue colours.

After shopping, Dimitri dropped me off and left for the mansion to talk to his father.

Dimitri's POV

I couldn't believe my ears. I was in the mansion. Valentina was here too. My mother talked to Valentina and asked her to give her money. 50.000$. I was frustrated. After all these years, she came back asking for money.

I ran my hand through my hair, trying to calm down.

"Dima, please calm down." Valentina said as she placed her hand on my arm.

"How? How can I?!" I snapped at her.

My father ended his call and walked towards us.

"Oleg searched. His husband lost plenty of money in poker and got bankrupt. He borrowed some many from someone, and they are after him." He informed.

"Mafia?" I asked. My father nodded.

I clenched my fist. She was back for her fucking bastard lover. I stood up.

"I am going home." I informed.

"Dima..."

I interrupted Valentina. "Not now, Valentina."

She nodded.

"See you later, son. And don't worry. I will handle it." My father said. I nodded and left.

When I arrived home, the living room was dark. I headed towards the bedroom.

Sarah was laying on the bed. When she saw me, she smiled at me. I smiled back and went towards the bed. I changed my clothes and lay down beside her on the bed and hugged her tightly.

"I missed you." I admitted as I smelt her heavenly scent and kissed her lips passionately.

I placed my head on her belly, rubbing it. She was stroking my hair.

"Do you want to talk about it?" She asked softly.

I sighed deeply and told her about everything.

"I am sorry, darling." She said.

I lifted my head up. "Don't be, it isn't your fault. Just hug me."

She nodded, smiling and hugged me. I wrapped my arms around her waist tightly and placed a soft kiss on her neck.

"Thank you for being beside me, kiska. I love you so much." I murmured, placing soft kisses on her neck.

"I love you too." She said, running her hands through my hair.

Chapter 19 - The visitor from the past

Sarah's POV

I hung up my phone and placed it into my bag. I was talking to my mother. She told me they would come before I gave birth. They had visited us twice after Dimitri and I got married. My mother liked Dimitri. She told me he was a charming man, and she was happy to see him being caring and affectionate towards me.

I walked into the bakery. I craved some croissants. The bakery smelled mouth-watering. After buying my croissant, I left the bakery.

As I walked away from the bakery a little, a man blocked my way. He was in his early thirties. He had black hair and brown eyes.

"Hey, beautiful." He smirked arrogantly.

I tried to pass by him, but he didn't let me as he grabbed my wrist.

"Let go of me!" I snapped, trying to pull my arm away.

He placed his free hand on my lower back as he leaned his face closer to me. I tried to push him back, but he tightened his grip, pulling me closer to him.

"Let go of me!" I shouted at him, frightened.

He tried to kiss me when I heard a familiar voice.

"Let go of her!"

It was Nikolai.

Thank God.

Nikolai grabbed his arm, pulling him away from me and punched his face. The man lost his balance and fell down.

"Are you okay?" Nikolai asked, concerned.

I just nodded. I couldn't talk. My legs were trembling.

The man ran away as soon as he stood up.

"Ok, come on. There is a cafe near here. You should pull yourself together. You look pale." He said and helped me to walk.

After drinking some water at the cafe, I felt a little better.

"Thank you, Nikolai. If you..." I couldn't hold my tears.

"Shh, okay. Everything is fine." He placed his hand on my arm, giving me a reassuring smile. "What were you doing here alone? It is dark outside. And you are pregnant. You shouldn't leave home alone at this hour. It is dangerous. Where is Dimitri?" He asked.

"He is in the mansion. He went to talk to his father. I wanted some crois-sants. So..." I murmured, rubbing my belly and shrugged my shoulders.

I shouldn't leave home at this hour. Dimitri hadn't let me leave home without the driver, but I didn't listen to him. Now I was regretting it. If he found out about what had happened, he would be frustrated.

"Nikolai, please....don't tell Dimitri. He will go mad." I muttered.

He gave me a warm smile and nodded. "I am sure about it." He chuckled. "But be more careful."

I smiled at him as I promised. "I will."

After Nikolai had dropped me off to the penthouse building, I thanked him again and walked into the penthouse building.

Dimitri's POV

I had a meeting early this morning. After getting ready, I looked at Sarah; she was sleeping peacefully. I kissed her forehead as I caressed her showing stomach and left.

After the meeting, I called my father. He was going to talk to my mother this morning.

"Hi, Dad."

"Hi, Dima. How are you, son? And Sarah?"

"Fine, Dad. She is fine too. Did you talk to her?"

He sighed. "Yeah. Don't worry. She will not bother us anymore."

"How?" I ran my fingers through my hair.

"I gave her the money she wanted. And probably, she is about to leave the country now."

"What?! Why, Dad? Why did you give her money? For that bastard?" I snapped. I was so angry.

"Dimitri, my children's happiness is important to me. And I know it is the only way. Trust me. She got what she wanted. She will not disturb us anymore."

I ran my hand through my hair, pacing back and forth in my office. I sighed deeply.

"Ok, Dad. If you think so." I murmured.

"Yes, Dima. Ok, I have to go to a meeting. But I will visit you this evening. I miss Sarah too."

"Ok. See you." I hung up and placed my phone down on the desk.

I sat down on my seat as I closed my eyes, holding my head in my hands.

My phone rang. I breathed deeply as I picked up the phone.

"Sir, you have a visitor." My secretary informed.

"Who?" I asked.

"Miss Alyona Antonova."

I breathed deeply, annoyed.

Another country heard from. I muttered under my breath.

"Sorry, sir?"

"Let her in."

A few seconds later, Alyona walked in. She wore a black ultra mini dress, showing her curves. She put her seductive smile on her face as she greeted me.

"Tell what you want and leave. I don't have so much time." I said dryly.

"You are so hospitable." She commented, smirking.

"Alyona, I am having a shitty day without you. Don't start you too." I snapped.

"Oh, my poor boy." She walked closer to me. When she wanted to stroke my hair, I pulled away and stood up.

"Alyona!" I hissed.

"Ok, ok. I have something important to tell you."

"I am all ears." I said sarcastically as I rolled my eyes.

"How is your precious wife?" She asked, emphasizing the last words.

I clenched my fist. "I will not repeat myself, Alyona. I don't have any time for your bullshit. Leave now!" I snapped.

"Do you know what your lovely wife is doing when you aren't around?" She asked sarcastically.

I raised my eyebrow at her. My jaw clenched. I breathed deeply.

"Don't push my patience!" I warned her and approached her. "Don't make me call securities."

She pulled an envelope out of her bag and handed me it.

I grabbed it angrily and opened it. There were photos in the envelope.

"See what your innocent wife is doing." She commented in a sarcastic voice.

When I looked at the photos, I was shocked. Sarah was in the arms of some bastard. They were too close like they were going to kiss.

My jaw tightened. My muscles tensed up as I was staring at the photos in my hand.

"Where did you find these photos?" I snarled.

"It isn't important." She replied, self-satisfied. "She isn't so innocent, is she?!" She added.

"Get out of here!" I barked as I grabbed her arm tightly, dragging her out.

"Dimitri, let go of me! You are hurting me." She shouted as she tried to pull her arm away to release my grip.

I threw her out of my office and slammed the door behind her.

I looked at the photos in my hand. I fisted my hand, crumbling them. I pounded my fist against the wall, cursing.

Chapter 20 - The disapointment

S arah's POV

I was waiting for Dimitri. I made dinner for us. I wanted to do something special for him. He had been feeling upset the past few days. I wanted to cherish him. I checked the table for the last time and went to the kitchen.

I heard noises coming from the living room. It must be Dimitri. I went to the living room.

"Hey, darling." I greeted him as I walked into the living room.

He gave me a cold glare. He looked so angry.

"Are you okay?" I asked as I approached him.

When I wanted to stroke his cheek, he held my wrist and pulled my hand away angrily.

"Dimitri, what is going on?" I asked, worried.

He gave me a sarcastic smile. "Are you worried about me? Aww, how thoughtful!" He said sarcastically.

I couldn't understand his attitude.

"Dimitri, is it your mother? Why are you angry?"

He laughed mockingly as he pulled something out of his pocket and threw on my face. The photos fell down. When I looked at them, I was shocked. There were the photos from that night. But the photos were taken from a different angle that showed like we were going to kiss. My heartbeats increased.

"I learned today that my wife is a slut. I think it is a good reason for being angry. What do you think, wifey?" He said, full of rage in his voice.

"Dimitri, this is not what it looks like. Please, let me explain." I pleaded, looking at him.

"You are like her. A cheap slut. I hate you. I hate you." He hissed as he approached me.

I couldn't believe my ears. He didn't trust me. A few photos were enough for him to think awful things about me. I felt disappointed.

He grabbed my arm tightly.

"This bastard is his. Am I right?! You fooled me. What were you two planning? To get money from me?" He barked, full of anger in his voice as he pointed to my bump.

I looked at him angrily. It was the last straw. How could he talk about our baby this way?! I slapped him.

His jaw clenched as he tightened his grip around my arm. I screamed in pain.

He looked at me frustrated. "Don't try it again, or you will regret it." He threatened me, emphasizing each word and dragged me with him.

"Let go of me! You are hurting me." I yelled, trying to get out of his grip.

"Get out of here! I don't want to see you nor your bastard!" He snapped as he dragged me out of the penthouse.

My eyes filled with tears. I sat down in front of the building. My legs were trembling; I couldn't stand anymore. I wrapped my arms around me, shaking. I was only in my dress; it was cold outside. My vision was blurry from tears. I leaned my back against the wall. I couldn't breathe properly.

"Sarah?" I lifted my gaze up as I heard Uncle Sergei's voice.

"Sarah, what happened? Why are you here alone? Oh my goodness! You are trembling." He said anxiously.

"Dimitri....." I muttered, trying to calm down.

"What has he done?" He asked furiously.

"Please, take me away from here." It was the only thing that I could say.

He sighed and nodded. He helped me to stand up. He took his coat off and placed it over my shoulders. I leaned against him for support. My legs were still trembling. He helped me to get in the car.

We were in the mansion. Finally, I could calm down a little, but I felt numb and tired. I told Uncle Sergei about everything.

Dimitri's POV

I was drinking my whiskey. I felt betrayed. I loved her. I was madly, deeply in love with her. But she....She fooled me, betrayed me.

My phone rang. I couldn't talk to someone now. I looked at the screen. It was my father. I didn't pick up my phone.

A few times later, finally, it stopped. But a few seconds later, he called again. I picked up the phone, breathing deeply.

"What?" I snapped.

"Come to the mansion immediately!" My father snarled.

"Dad, I am not..."

"Dimitri, come here immediately!" He barked and hung up.

I breathed deeply and stood up as I grabbed my phone. I left the penthouse.

When I walked into the mansion, I saw Sarah sitting on the couch in the living room. I clenched my fist. My blood was boiling.

"What the hell is this whore doing here?" I snapped.

"Dimitri! Watch your language!" My father demanded.

"I am leaving. I don't want to see her face anymore."

"Dimitri! That is enough!" My father snapped. "You should listen to Sarah." He added softly.

I gave him a fake smirk. "I think I heard her lies enough." I said bitterly. I looked at her. "And you, you can fool my father with your lies but not me. Get out of my life. I don't want to see you. Do you get it?" I snapped angrily.

"Dimitri! She is pregnant. At least...."

I laughed as I interrupted my father. "I am not interested in her nor her bastard."

"Dimitri!" My father slapped me.

I placed my hand on my cheek. I clenched my fist. I was holding myself hard.

Sarah's POV

I couldn't believe my ears. It must have been a nightmare. I couldn't say anything; I felt bad.

Uncle Sergei slapped him. His jaw clenched. He looked frustrated like a wild animal. He rubbed his cheek as he looked at me, full of frustration in his eyes.

"Leave, Dimitri! You should calm down." His father said.

His eyes were still glued to my eyes. He looked at me like he wanted to jump down on my throat.

"Fuck with you!" He snapped as he pointed his finger at me.

"Dimitri!" His father warned him.

He left the mansion, slamming the door behind him.

I felt dizzy. I couldn't breathe properly anymore. I tried to control my breaths.

Suddenly, I felt a sharp pain in my stomach. I screamed in pain and placed my hand on my stomach.

"Sarah!" Uncle Sergei approached me. He looked at me, worried. "What happened?" He asked anxiously.

I felt another pain as I wanted to reply. I wrapped my arms around my stomach in pain, screaming.

Chapter 21 - Regret

S arah's POV

When I opened my eyes, I was in the hospital. The last thing that I had remembered was we were going to the hospital. Then, I must have fainted.

"Sarah, how do you feel?" Uncle Sergei asked, worried.

I placed my hand on my stomach anxiously.

"My baby?" I asked, trying to sit up.

"He is fine. Don't worry." He replied tenderly. "You should rest. Lie down. The doctor will come." He added.

I nodded. I was so worried about my baby. If something happened to him, I wouldn't forgive Dimitri nor myself.

A few minutes later, the doctor walked in.

"Sarah, how do you feel now?" She asked.

"Better. Is my baby fine?" I wanted to be sure.

"...There is the risk of premature birth. And it is dangerous for the baby. You should avoid everything that causes you stress, and lie as much as possible without standing so long." The doctor informed.

Dimitri's POV

My father called me again. I hadn't been picking up his calls. I turned off my phone. I didn't want to hear anything about Sarah.

I poured whiskey for myself again.

The elevator door opened.

"Hey, Dima." Nikolai walked in.

"Hey." I muttered. "Would you like to drink something?" I asked, pointing to my glass.

He nodded. I poured whiskey for him and handed him the glass as I sat down on the couch.

He sipped his drink as he was looking around.

"Looking for someone?" I asked sarcastically.

Nikolai raised his eyebrow curiously. "How is Sarah?"

Finally, he spilled the beans. Sarah. Sarah. The name that had made my heart melt before, but now it was just irritating me.

"To hell with her." I snapped carelessly and sipped my drink.

He looked at me, puzzled. Then, he shook his head, sighing.

"What have you done again?" He asked, annoyed.

Me? Why does everybody think that it is me who does bad things? Of course, she is an angel without wings.

I tightened my grip around my glass. My jaw clenched.

"I did nothing. Your precious angel cheated on me with some bastard." I barked angrily.

He looked at me, trying to understand what I had told. Then, he burst out laughing.

"Really?!" He said mockingly.

I looked at him with a grave glare. He stopped laughing.

"What the hell are you talking about, Dima? Are you drunk?"

I closed my eyes as I breathed in deeply. I stood up and went towards the drawer. I pulled the photos out of the drawer and extended the photos to him. He took the photos and looked at them attentively. Then, a smile appeared on his face.

"Is it all?" He asked, shaking the photos in his hand.

I raised my eyebrow. "Isn't it enough?" I asked mockingly. "Don't you see it?!"

"I see and know what has happened there because I was there too."

I looked at him, puzzled.

He breathed in deeply, and he told me about that night. I couldn't believe my ears. I was shocked as well as happy. I hated myself.

Damn it! What the hell have I done? I totally screwed up.

"Shit! Shit!" I hissed.

"Where did you find these photos?" He asked.

"Alyona." I replied and sighed.

He rolled his eyes, annoyed.

"Really, Dima?! I thought you were wise. You don't know her?! She is capable of doing everything to get into your bed again. Damn it!"

"I know. I know. But when I saw these photos, I got fucking jealous. I felt betrayed. I couldn't think properly. Thinking someone touched her, kissed her...." I shook my head. "I fucked up. I told her awful things." I ran my hand through my hair. "Even I told her that the baby isn't mine." I felt awful thinking what I had told her.

"What?! Dima how could you think that she...." He stopped without finishing his sentence, shaking his head with a disapproving look on his face.

"Where is she now?" He asked.

"In the mansion. My father saw her in front of the building last night...after I have thrown her out." I replied, feeling guilty.

Nikolai clenched his jaw.

"I am holding myself hard not to punch you, dude." He admitted.

"I will not stop you if you do. Trust me." I confessed.

I grabbed my phone and turned on it. My phone buzzed again and again.

Pick up the damn phone, Dimitri!

Dimitri, it is important. Call me.

We are in the hospital. Sarah felt bad.

My eyes widened. Immediately, I called him.

Please, God, don't let anything happen to them.

"What happened, Dima?" Nikolai asked, worried.

"Sarah.. She is in the hospital." I responded as I grabbed my jacket.

I headed towards the elevator.

"I am coming too." Nikolai followed me.

Finally, my father picked up the phone.

"Dad, how is Sarah? Is the baby fine?" I asked anxiously.

"Finally, they come into your mind." He replied bitterly.

"Dad! How are they? Please, tell me. Where are you now? Which hospital?" I asked, devastated as Nikolai and I got in my car.

My father told me the address. I hung up the phone as I was speeding up.

Finally, we arrived at the hospital. I rushed towards her room. Nikolai followed me. I walked into the room.

"Sarah. Are you okay? How is our baby? I was fucking worried." I said anxiously as I placed my hand on the top of her hand on her stomach.

She pulled her hand away.

"Our baby? Did you lose your memory? The last time I had checked you were shouting that he was not yours, calling him bastard." She said bitterly, looking at me with pure anger and sadness in her eyes.

"Sarah, I am sorry. I felt jealous and betrayed. I couldn't think properly."

"You should trust me. I am your damn wife! But you preferred to believe those damn photos!" She yelled at me. "Now, leave! Get out of here! I don't want to see your face. I hate you. I hate you." She shouted at me.

"Sarah..."

"Get out of here!"

"Dimitri, leave, please. And you Sarah, calm down. Please, remember what the doctor has said." My father intervened.

"Dad..."

He placed his hand on my shoulder, pulling me out with him. I walked out. I ran my hand through my hair angrily.

"Damn it!" I hissed as I punched the wall.

Chapter 22 - Old habits

D imitri's POV

"Dimitri, calm down!" My father demanded.

"How?!" I barked. "How?! When the woman who I love desperately hates me." I added.

"You should leave. Both of you need to calm down." He commented.

"No! I am not going anywhere." I protested.

"Dima, she doesn't want to see you now."

"I will not leave, Dad. I will stay beside her and my baby."

"She has the risk of premature birth." My father informed.

"What?" I asked, terrified.

"The doctor said that it is dangerous for the baby. She should stay away from stress. Do you understand me? Now leave. When she accepts to see you, I will inform you."

"No, Dad....I can not leave them alone. I want to be beside them." I said desperately.

"Dimitri, she doesn't want to see you. And I will do everything to protect my grandchild. Even if the cost is that I keep you away from them."

"You can not do it. They are my family. My wife and my son." I snapped.

"Then, think about their health."

I frowned, running my hand through my hair angrily.

I stormed out of the hospital. I got in my car. Nikolai got in my car too.

"Get out of the car!" I barked.

"No. I can not leave you alone when you are in this state. Where are you going?"

"To kill someone." I snapped as I started the car.

I parked the car in front of Alyona's building. I got out of the car and rushed into the apartment building. Nikolai came after me, calling me, but I didn't stop.

I was banging on the door.

"Open the damn door, Alyona!" I shouted.

As soon as she opened the door, I barged in as I strangled her throat, pushing her back against the wall. She was trying to release my grip. Her face got red.

"Dimitri, stop! You are going to kill her." Nikolai shouted as he was trying to pull me away, but I tightened my grip around her throat.

"Dimitri!" Nikolai pulled me away.

Alyona slid down against the wall as she held her throat, choking.

"Give me his address, or I will kill you!" I barked at her.

Nikolai was standing between us, placing his hands on my chest, trying to keep me away from her.

"Tell me!" I shouted.

"Let go of me, Nikolai!" I pushed him away and approached her. I grabbed her arm tightly.

"Who is that bastard? I know about your plan. I will kill you and him." I was shaking her.

"Dimitri, please...." She begged.

"Tell me!"

"Oleg, my cousin."

After she had given me his address, I left her house.

As soon as that bastard opened the door, I punched him. He lost his balance and fell down. I started to hit his stomach.

Nikolai pulled me back. "Dimitri, stop!"

"Nikolai, don't intervene. I will kill him." I barked, looking at the man laying on the floor, bleeding.

Nikolai dragged me out.

"Stop! That is enough."

I breathed deeply. "My son can...." I muttered, closing my eyes. "Because of them!"

"I know, but you should calm down. Sarah and your son need you. Beside them, not in the jail." He tapped my shoulder. "Now, give me your car key. I will drop you off. You drive like crazy, I want to live." He chuckled.

Sarah's POV

When I opened my eyes, the sun was shining through the windows. I was in the mansion. I left the hospital this morning. I sat up on the bed and rubbed my stomach.

I saw my suitcase in the bedroom. Yesterday, I told Uncle Sergei that I wouldn't go back to the penthouse. I wasn't ready to see Dimitri's face nor hear his voice. Uncle Sergei said he was going to send someone to bring me some clothes and personal stuff.

I stood up and went to the bathroom. After taking a shower, I put my clothes on. Then I went downstairs.

When I was about to go to the living room, I saw Nikolai sitting on the couch. When he saw me, he stood up as he greeted me.

"Hi." I greeted him as I sat down on the couch. He joined me.

"How do you feel?" He asked, concerned.

"I am fine. Thanks."

"Olga is worried about you too. She wanted to come, but the babysitter has day off. She couldn't let our daughter alone."

"Don't worry. I am fine. How is your daughter? " I asked, giving him a slight smile.

"She is fine. Thanks." He cleared his throat and said. "Umm...Dimitri..."

"Nikolai, please. I don't want to hear anything about him." I interrupted him.

"Sarah, I know you are angry at him, and you are right. But he feels bad. He really regrets what he has done. It is Alyona. She planned all of these."

I raised my eyebrow at him with an inquiring look. "Alyona?"

He told me about everything. Now my anger had doubled. He trusted his ex-girlfriend more than his wife.

"He was like a wild animal yesterday. I barely hold him back. If I wasn't with him yesterday, he probably would be in a jail now. He barged in her house. As he strangled her, I intervened. Then, he went to her cousin's house and beat him. That bastard's face was totally in blood. And the last time I had checked, he was telling his men to banish them from the city to Siberia." He said with an amused smile, shaking his head.

"Oh..Sarah. You are here." Uncle Sergei walked toward us.

After having lunch together, I went to the bathroom. When I was coming back to the living room, I heard Nikolai and Uncle Sergei talking.

"Doesn't he pick up your call too?" Uncle Sergei asked.

"No." Nikolai sighed.

"Ugh. This boy will be the death of me." Uncle Sergei said, annoyed.

"Don't worry, Uncle. Probably, he is drinking somewhere." Nikolai commented, trying to reassure him.

Probably, they were talking about Dimitri. Despite my anger, I got worried about him.

Where is he?

"I am afraid that he will go back to his damn friends and his previous habits." Uncle Sergei said, worried.

I didn't understand.

What habits? What are they talking about?

Chapter 23 - The bad boy

Sarah's POV

"No, I don't think so. But if you want, I will call Igor." Nikolai suggested.

"Call him."

After talking a while, Nikolai hung up and informed. "They are meeting up tonight."

"I knew. What will I do with that boy?" Uncle Sergei hissed.

I couldn't eavesdrop anymore, I went beside them. When they saw me, they stopped talking.

"What happened? Where is Dimitri?" I asked, worried.

They looked at each other.

"I heard what you were talking about." I added. "What habits?" I asked.

Uncle Sergei sighed. Nikolai looked at him like he was waiting for his approval. Uncle Sergei nodded.

"Illegal motorcycle races." Nikolai answered as he looked at me.

What?

"He had an accident a few years ago. After the accident, he promised he would not do it again. But... " He shrugged his shoulders.

Ugh. Real asshole. He didn't even let me be angry at him. I was worried about him now.

"Do you know where the race will be?" I asked. He nodded.

"Ok. I will grab my bag, and we will go there." I said.

"No!" They both stated at the same time.

"You heard what the doctor had said. No stress. You aren't going anywhere. Especially there." Uncle Sergei demanded.

"But..."

"Sarah, I said no. End of the discussion." He stated confidently. "Don't worry. I am going there, and I will bring him. I will not allow him to make the same mistakes." He added. "Nikolai, let's go." Then, he looked at Nikolai as he said. Nikolai nodded, and they left afterwards.

Dimitri's POV

I put on my helmet and got on my motorcycle. As I sped up, I felt carefree. I needed to drift away all of these. I wanted to shut my mind off. At least, for tonight.

I stopped beside Igor. I gave him a side hug.

"Are you ready?" He asked, smirking.

"As always." I winked, giving him an arrogant smirk.

"Someone missed you too." He commented, smirking, looking at a girl standing far away.

"Alina?"

"Yes, she has been asking about you."

"I am not interested." I confirmed dryly.

"Dima!" Alina called me as she approached me, smiling seductively.

"Hey." I muttered.

She placed her hand on my arm. "Where have you been? I missed you." She said in a seductive voice, caressing my arm with her fingertips slowly.

I cleared my throat as I pulled my arm away.

"Let's start." I suggested as I looked at Igor, ignoring Alina. She scowled and walked away.

Finally!

When I wanted to put on my helmet, I heard my name.

Shit! I hissed as I saw two familiar people coming towards me.

"What the hell are you doing here?!" My father snapped.

"Hi, Dad. I am bad. And you?" I said mockingly.

He rolled his eyes. "Dimitri, stop it. You promised that you would stay away from this shit."

I sighed as I ran my hands through my hair.

"Dad, you stop. It is my life. Mind your own business!" I stated angrily.

"Dimitri!" He hissed.

"What?! My own wife hates me. My own father doesn't let me come near my wife to make her forgive me...." I hissed.

Nikolai intervened as he said. "Dimitri, think about Sarah and your baby. She is worried about you. You know what the doctor has said about her situation."

"Don't worry. She is busy with hating me now." I commented dryly. Even this thought made my heart sink.

"Are you sure?! We stopped her hard. She wanted to come here when she found out about this shit. That you put your life in danger. You dumbass! She loves you."

Really?

I smiled with happiness.

She still loves me.

I had hope now. I would do everything for her forgiveness.

"Now, let's go." Nikolai suggested. I nodded.

Sarah's POV

When I woke up, there was a beautiful bouquet on the table. Beautiful pink roses as I loved. The smell of the roses filled the bedroom.

I got up, smiling and put on my silk robe as I walked closer towards the roses. I took the bouquet and smelt the roses, closing my eyes. When I reopened my eyes, I noticed a note on it.

'I hurt you, and it's killing me. I am so sorry. Give me a chance. I promise I will do everything to make you happy. Please, forgive this idiot. I love you so much. Dimitri.'

I smiled as I read the note, but I couldn't forgive him so easily. He scattered my heart. I was so disappointed in him.

I placed the roses down on the table and went to change my clothes.

In the evening, Uncle Sergei, Valentina and I were having dinner. The mansion was filled with pink roses. Dimitri had sent roses all day long. Uncle Sergei said that he didn't let him come to the mansion. And added that he would only give permission if I would want it. I hadn't been ready to talk to him yet. But seeing his attention, how he was trying to make me forgive him, made me happy. At least, I knew he was sorry for his behavior as he should be.

The doorbell hummed.

The housekeeper brought a big boutique to the living room.

"This boy turned my home into Dimitri's botanic garden." Uncle Sergei commented playfully as he shook his head.

Valentina and I burst out laughing. Uncle Sergei was really right. The living room was filled with roses like it was a flower shop or garden.

Chapter 24 - Rainy welcome

Sarah's POV

I was nine months pregnant now. Yesterday, I had a doctor appointment, she told me that my baby was healthy, and there was not any danger for him anymore. I was relieved. I was so afraid that something could happen to my little boy.

I walked towards the window while I was caressing my swollen bump. I saw Dimitri in the garden, sitting on the bonnet of his car.

Dimitri had been waiting for me in front of the mansion. Uncle Sergei hadn't still let him in. But he was here every day without getting bored. It made me feel happy and precious. He sent flowers, chocolate, jewelry. He called me every day, but I didn't pick up his calls nor go to see him in the garden.

When Dimitri lifted his head up, our eyes met. He smiled at me sadly. His every glare made my heart melt, but I was being so stubborn towards him. I wanted to run to him and hug him tightly, kissing his lips, but my pride was not letting me do it. I missed him so much. His touches, the warmth of his skin, his mind-blowing scent and more.

I walked away from the window. Suddenly, I felt a sharp pain in my stomach. I squeezed my lips together, putting my hand on my stomach. I felt sharp pains a few times today. The doctor said it was normal, because my due date was so close. A few seconds later, it passed. I went downstairs.

This evening Uncle Sergei had a dinner meeting.

As he hung up his phone, he asked. "Sarah, how do you feel?"

"I am fine. Don't worry." I replied, giving him a reassuring smile.

"It is an important meeting. I can not change. But if you feel bad, call me immediately." He said seriously. "And I am a little relaxed, because your loyal bodyguard is outside." He added, smirking. I smiled back as I nodded. Then, he left.

It was raining. When I had checked the last time, Dimitri was still here. He was waiting in his car. I was worried about him; today the weather was so cold. At least, he was in his car now. I sighed.

I stood up and walked towards the window. He was still here. Finally, I decided to go and tell him that he should leave.

I put on my leather jacket and took my umbrella. I walked out.

When he saw me, he got out of his car quickly and walked towards me under rain while getting wet in the rain.

As he approached me, he asked nervously, placing his hand on my stomach. "Are you okay? Do you feel bad? Do you have contractions?"

I sighed as I replied. "I am fine, Dimitri. I come here to tell you that you should leave. It is cold outside as well as raining. You will catch a cold."

He smiled at me with his signature smirk. "Are you worried about me, kiska?" He asked, caressing my baby bump.

I breathed deeply. I regretted coming here.

"I shouldn't come." I commented as I turned around.

He grabbed my arm. "Please." He muttered, giving me a begging look. "I am sorry, Sarah. I am really sorry. I acted like a jerk. But when I saw...those photos, I got mad. I was so jealous and felt betrayed. I was so blinded by my anger." He confessed sadly.

I gave him a fake smile. "You believed your ex-girlfriend more than me, Dimitri. You didn't even let me explain."

"Sarah...I didn't believe her. Please, believe me. I am so sorry. I love you so much." He begged.

"It is not important anymore." As I wanted to leave, I felt a sharp pain in my stomach.

I screamed in pain, placing my hand on my stomach.

"What? What happened? Are you okay?" Dimitri asked, terrified as he wrapped his arm around me.

Suddenly, I felt water running down my legs.

"My water..." I said in panic, looking down at my legs, my eyes wide.

Dimitri's eyes widened; his face got pale.

"Ok....calm down....We are going to the hospital." He stated, trying to control his voice.

I nodded as I squeezed his hand when I felt another sharp pain.

He led us towards his car.

"My maternity bag." I mentioned barely.

He nodded as he called the security guard. The security guard rushed towards us.

"Bring her maternity bag." Dimitri ordered. He nodded and rushed towards the door.

Dimitri helped me to get in the car. He closed the door for me and got in the car as soon as he took the bag from the security guard.

I was inhaling and exhaling deeply. It was hurting so much.

He started the car. He was driving fast while he was trying to support me, breathing with me.

Finally, we arrived. He got out of his car quickly and opened the door. He scooped me up in his arms bridal style, and he carried me inside. He put me on the stretcher and held my hand. I was squeezing his hand tightly as I felt pain.

The nurse took me to the room. Dimitri was waiting for me outside. The doctor walked in.

Dimitri's POV

They took her into the room. I was waiting outside. I was worried about them. I was pacing back and forth nervously.

Finally, the doctor walked out. I approached her.

"How is she?" I asked anxiously.

"She is in labor. We are taking her to the delivery room." She informed me.

I was waiting in front of the delivery room, leaning against the wall. I folded my arms over my chest.

"Dimitri." My father called me, as he approached me. "What have you done now?!" He snapped at me.

"We were just talking when her water broke. I swear, Dad." I informed.

"Yes, she felt pain this morning too." He softened.

I ran my hand through my hair, closing my eyes shut. I felt a hand on my shoulder.

"They will be fine. Don't worry, son." My father assured as he gave me a reassuring smile.

"I hope so." I said, biting my lower lip nervously.

Chapter 25 - Little prince

- -

Dimitri's POV

A few hours had passed, but there was no news from the delivery room. I was so worried.

"Why don't they say anything?" I asked nervously as I slammed my fist against the wall.

"Dimitri, calm down." My father said, putting his hand on my shoulder.

"Dimitri, Dad, how are Sarah and the baby?" Valentina asked as she and her husband approached us.

"We are still waiting." My father replied.

Valentina hugged me. I hugged her back.

She pulled back and handed me a bag.

"Dad told me to bring you clean clothes. Go and change. Don't worry, if there is the news, we will tell you."

I nodded as I took the bag. I was still in my wet clothes.

I changed my clothes quickly in the room and went back. We were still waiting, sitting beside the delivery room.

Finally, the doctor walked out. I stood up quickly and approached her.

"How are they?" I asked nervously.

"Congratulations, Mr. Fedorov. The baby was born. The mother and baby are healthy." She informed, smiling.

"Oh, thank God." I sighed, relieved, placing my hands on my face, my eyes closed. "I am a father." I commented happily.

"Congratulations, son." My father hugged me. I hugged him back.

My eyes filled with tears of happiness and joy. Then, I hugged Valentina, her husband.

The nurse walked out, holding my son in her arms. She smiled at me as she gave me my son.

My little bundle of joy.

I took him in my arms carefully.

"Hey, my little prince. Welcome to our life." I whispered, kissing his chubby cheek.

He was so tiny that I was afraid of hurting him. It was one of the best feelings in the world. Holding my son in my arms. My own flesh and blood. It was the best gift that someone could receive.

"Daddy loves you, little prince." I said, looking at him, mesmerized.

"Aww, he is so cute." Valentina commented, caressing his little hand.

"I need to take him for a check up." The nurse interrupted us. I nodded and gave her my son.

Then, the door opened and they brought Sarah. I approached her and held her hand as I placed a soft kiss on her forehead.

"Thank you, kiska. You made me the happiest man on earth. I love you. I love you so much." I said as I wiped my tears off my cheeks.

"Dimitri. I love you, too. " She admitted, making me double happy. I was on cloud nine. She forgave me.

My woman. My Sarah. The mother of my son. The only love of my life. My everything. My breath in the fresh air.

Sarah's POV

I was in the room, waiting for my little boy. Everybody was beside me. Dimitri was sitting beside me, holding my hand.

Finally, the door opened, and the nurse walked in, holding our son.

I was so nervous and happy. She gave me my son. I held him in my arms.

"My little boy." I whispered, kissing his cheek.

"He is so cute. He will be so handsome." Valentina commented, looking at my son.

"Of course. As his father." Dimitri stated with a cocky grin on his face.

Everyone laughed.

"But not as arrogant as him." I added amusingly.

"Hey!" Dimitri raised his eyebrow at me playfully.

A few hours later, we were alone. Dimitri, our boy and I. Dimitri was sitting beside me on the bed, wrapping his arm around my shoulder. My boy was sleeping in my arms.

"But it is unfair. He totally looks like you." I admitted. "At least, look like your mother a little, my baby." I added, caressing my little boy's cheek with my fingertip.

He had blond hair and emerald green eyes as his father's. His chin, lips, nose looked like him.

"Of course, he will be. I worked hard at making him." Dimitri commented arrogantly and winked at me.

"Pervert!" I exclaimed, laughing.

"I love you, kiska." He murmured as he kissed my lips.

"I love you, too." I said and brushed my lips against his lips.

Today we were leaving the hospital. I put on a navy blue dress and leather jacket. Andrei, my little boy was sleeping in his crib peacefully. We were waiting for Dimitri. He was signing some papers to leave the hospital.

I held Andrei in my arms carefully without waking him up and placed him in his baby car seat. I pulled a blanket over him.

"Are you ready?" Dimitri asked as he walked in.

"Yes." I replied.

He took the baby car seat and held my hand. We walked out.

After I got in the car, Dimitri placed the baby car seat beside me and closed the door for me. He got in the car and started the car after giving me a tender smile through the rear view mirror. I smiled at him back.

He parked his car in front of the penthouse building. He got out of the car quickly and opened the door for me. He took the baby car seat. I got out of the car. He held my hand as we walked towards the building.

As the elevator door opened, everyone greeted us, cheering. Everyone was here: Uncle Sergei, Valentina, her husband, their daughter, my parents, my brother, Galina.

The living room was decorated with blue balloons, the banner "Welcome home, Andrei." had written on it, blue and golden confetti. There were a lot of adorable cupcakes, cakes and so on.

After spending some time together, Dimitri and I took our boy to his nursery room. We had prepared his room before our fight. The room was decorated in blue, white and golden colours. It looked elegant, joyful and calming.

I placed Andrei in his crib carefully. He was sleeping peacefully. I pulled a blanket over him.

Dimitri wrapped his arms around my waist from behind as he rested his chin on my shoulder.

"I love you, kiska." He murmured in my ear as he planted a soft kiss on my neck.

Chapter 26 - New life

Sarah's POV

I was in our bedroom when Dimitri walked in, giving me a warm smile. I noticed a velvet box in his hand.

He walked closer to me and opened the box.

"To the best and beautiful mother in the world." He said, looking at me tenderly.

There was a beautiful necklace in the box. Pear-shaped morganite, baguette pink tourmalines and round brilliant diamonds, set in platinum. It was so elegant and sophisticated.

"Dimitri...it is so beautiful." I commented, looking at the necklace.

"You are more beautiful." He said. "Let me put it on you."

I nodded and pulled my hair to the side.

He stood behind me and put on the necklace on my neck.

"Perfect!" He exclaimed, looking at me in the mirror.

"Thank you." I gave him a bright smile.

He placed a soft kiss on my neck.

We changed our clothes and lay down on the bed. I placed my head on his chest while he wrapped his arm around me.

"I missed holding you in my arms. These last weeks without you have been the worst days in my life. I will never let you go again, kiska." He confessed and placed a tender kiss on my forehead.

"I missed you, too." I admitted.

When I walked out of the bathroom, I saw Dimitri in the bedroom changing Andrei's diaper.

He was making different funny faces while he was cleaning Andrei. I leaned against the door frame while watching them. They were so cute together.

Suddenly, Andrei peed on Dimitri's face. I burst out laughing.

He pulled back quickly as he wiped his face with tissue.

"Hey, don't laugh." He demanded, looking at me.

"Sorry..." I couldn't finish my sentence and started laughing again. "But it is funny." I added, laughing.

He gave me a dirty look and looked down at our son.

"Hey, little prince, don't put your father in shame. You are a good boy, aren't you?" He cooed Andrei.

I walked closer to them as I offered. "Let me help you."

"No, we will manage." He refused, looking at our son.

"Done!" He exclaimed as he held our son in his arms and put a soft kiss on his cheek.

"You are the best father in the world." I commented and kissed Dimitri's cheek, giving him an admiring look.

As I was breastfeeding our son, Dimitri walked closer to me.

"I have a surprise for you." He informed happily.

I raised my eyebrow with an inquiring look. "What surprise?"

"I will not tell you. Get ready. Galina will look after Andrei."

I nodded in agreement.

After finishing breastfeeding Andrei, I gave Dimitri our son and went to our bedroom.

I put on a pencil black skirt and wine red blouse. I did my hair wavy and applied light makeup. I took my bag and leather jacket and left the bedroom.

Dimitri was waiting for me in the living room.

He looked at me from head to toe with salacious eyes.

"These weeks are not going to be easy." He confessed, biting his lower lip as he wrapped his arm around me, pulling me closer to him.

I kissed his lips. When I wanted to pull back, he tightened his grip around me, pulling me closer as he plunged his tongue inside my mouth, kissing me passionately.

"How long should we wait?" He asked as he pulled his lips back.

"The doctor said we should wait six weeks." I informed.

He sighed. I smiled at his reaction and kissed his lips as I caressed his cheek affectionately.

He held my hand and placed a soft kiss on my palm. Then, he entwined our fingers and led us towards the elevator.

He stopped his car in front of a mansion. He got out of the car and approached my side. He opened the door for me and extended his hand towards me.

"Dimitri, where are we? What are we doing here?" I asked curiously as I held his hand.

"A little patience, kiska." He replied as we walked towards the mansion.

"Who lives here?" I asked while watching the garden as we walked towards the mansion.

He wrapped his arms around me. "Us. If you like it." He responded.

"What?" I asked, surprised.

"It is our house. I bought it for us: You, our children and me." He replied, excited, caressing my cheek, emphasizing the word children.

"Do you like it?" He asked.

"I love it. Thank you. It is so beautiful." I said happily as I hugged him. He hugged me back.

"Let's see inside." He suggested. I nodded.

The mansion was approached by a substantial tree-lined driveway which sits behind a gated entrance. The stylish stucco home had a modest entrance, which was purposefully designed to dramatically expand as you entered the home; stepping into a palatial building with a grand entrance equipped with a sweeping staircase and direct open views of the southern portion of the grounds. The floor plan was balanced across three principal wings: chef's kitchen, another hosting a distinguished library, the third bearing several staff/guest rooms with a separate entrance.

The mansion maintained many of its original features, including molded ceilings with traditional chandeliers, Italian marble fireplaces, French parquet floors, and antique bathroom fixtures.

The interior of the home bore the grace of traditional elegance, with soaring ceilings and huge windows throughout. The main living spaces included a living room, a family room, a game room, recreation rooms, and two master suites. Aside from the main house, the property also included a separate carriage house which had three bedrooms and a bathroom, and a detached six-car garage.

The large outdoor pool area was perfectly sited with a gentle hedged-border and features multiple dining and entertaining areas, complete with a swimming pool, separate spa, full outdoor kitchen, and shower. The outdoor recreational areas included a tennis court and a basketball court. The property bore verdant landscaping including mature trees and sprawling lawns, with multiple lush gardens.

"I hired an interior designer for the mansion. Tomorrow we have a meeting with her. I want to decorate it as you wish." He confirmed.

"Thank you, Dimitri." I kissed his lips.

"All pleasure is mine." He said and kissed me again.

Epilogue

A year later

Sarah's POV

Today was Andrei's birthday. We were celebrating his birthday in our mansion. Everything was ready: a cake, different cupcakes, balloons, other decorations.

As I went to the garden, I saw Dimitri and Andrei playing.

Dimitri caught him and started tickling him. Andrei was giggling while trying to pull away. Dimitri kissed his cheek and took him in his arms.

I approached them and caressed my little prince's chubby cheek.

Dimitri wrapped his free arm around my shoulder while he was holding Andrei in his arm, pulling me closer to him and brushed his lips against mine.

"Hi." Our parents and Valentina with her family greeted us as they walked towards us.

Valentina had another child two months ago. He was a cute boy.

My brother could not come. He got married eight months ago. His wife was pregnant with their first child. The doctor did not let her fly on the plane.

After blowing up candles on the cake, Andrei was busy with opening his gifts. Most correctly, tearing gift papers impatiently. Dimitri was helping him to open the gifts.

After opening all the gifts, they started playing with toys. Dimitri was as happy as Andrei while playing with a remote control helicopter.

Boys never grow up.

After everyone had left, we put Andrei in his crib. He fell asleep immediately. My little boy got so tired today; he played and ran in the garden all day long.

As Dimitri walked into our bedroom, he looked at me from head to toe lustfully. I wore a navy blue silk nightie.

"You are stunning." He stated, emphasizing each word as he approached me.

He wrapped his arms around me, pulling me closer to him and brushed his lips against mine. He plunged his tongue inside my mouth while he slid his hand under my nightie, rubbing my thigh. I moaned, gripping his hair.

He was kissing me hungrily while leading us towards the bed.

As my back touched the bed, I started to unbutton his shirt while he was kissing my neck. I took his shirt off and ran my hands along his bare back. He took my nightie off.

He trailed his lips down to my breast and put my nipple into his mouth. He started torturing me with his expert tongue. A loud moan escaped from my lips.

He trailed his lips down, placing soft kisses. I closed my eyes, enjoying his touches. Then, he stopped as he reached my panties and took my panties off in a flash. He gave me a devilish smirk before kissing me between my legs, making me gasp in pleasure.

He was torturing me with his tongue and fingers.

"Dimitri." I moaned, squeezing my eyes shut as I came.

He took his boxer off and parted my legs apart, positioning himself between my legs. He shoved his length inside me. I gasped, squeezing the sheet tightly. He entwined our hands above my head and rejoined our lips in a passionate kiss as he started moving inside me.

He screamed my name out as he came inside me. He collapsed on top of me. We were panting.

He rolled over and pulled me into his embrace.

"I love you, kiska." He said as he placed a tender kiss on my lips.

"I love you, too." I admitted, closing my eyes.

The next morning I woke up feeling nauseous. I put on my nightie quickly and ran to the bathroom, covering my mouth with my hand.

After vomiting, I brushed my teeth and washed my face. My face was still pale. I had been vomiting the last few weeks.

"Sarah." I heard Dimitri's voice.

"Coming." I left the bathroom.

Dimitri was in the bedroom, holding Andrei in his arms. Andrei was sobbing.

"He must be hungry. Galina is making breakfast. Can you hold him? I have a meeting early in the morning. I have to get ready." He said.

I nodded and took Andrei in my arms.

"My little prince, we are going to eat." I cooed him, caressing his silky blond hair. He cuddled in my arms, placing his head on my chest.

"I will pick you up at 7.00 p.m. Be ready." Dimitri informed while putting on his black suit pants.

I nodded. We were going to the restaurant this evening.

I put on a black midi dress and did my hair wavy. After putting my makeup, I took my clutch and left.

Dimitri stopped his car in front of the restaurant. We got out of his car. He placed his hand on my lower back and led us towards the entrance.

After the restaurant, we went for a walk.

We were walking along the Neva River, holding each other's hand.

"Do you remember when we were here for the first time?" Dimitri asked, wrapping his arm around me.

"How I can forget. It was a magnificent view. And my encounter was so handsome. As he is now, too." I replied, smiling happily.

He smiled at me back and planted a tender kiss on my lips.

Suddenly, my head spun. Dimitri caught me by my waist without letting me fall.

"Kiska, are you okay?" He asked nervously.

Without managing to reply my vision darkened.

When I opened my eyes, I was in the hospital. Dimitri was beside me, holding my hand.

When he noticed that I opened my eyes, he asked, worried. "How do you feel, kiska?" He was caressing my hair.

"What happened?"

"You fainted. I was so worried." He replied and placed a soft kiss on my forehead.

The door opened. The doctor walked in.

After asking how I felt, she informed. "Congratulations, you are two months pregnant."

"What?!" Dimitri looked at me, surprised. "We are having a baby again." He commented with happiness and joy in his eyes as he hugged me. I hugged him back happily.

Two years later

Sarah's POV

I was waiting for Dimitri, holding our little daughter, Mila in my arms. We were in New York to visit my parents. Dimitri went to buy some coffee for us with Andrei. From the same coffee shop that I bumped into him when I left this coffee shop.

"Mrs. Federova, your coffee." Dimitri said with an arrogant smirk on his face like the first day when we met while he was holding Andrei's hand.

I took the cup. "Thank you, Mr. Federov."

"Everything started with coffee." He commented as he wrapped his arm around me. "You turned my whole world upside down after my eyes laid on you." He added.

"I don't think so. You just wanted me to get into your bed and make your father angry." I stated.

"But I was a gentleman. Don't forget when you were drunk and jumped on me without resisting my irresistible charm anymore, I didn't touch you." He reminded, giving me an arrogant smirk.

"Yes. But I have some suspicion about it that you did it to earn my trust. It was a high percentage play." I commented.

"You broke my heart." He faked a sad expression, placing his hand on his heart.

I gave him a knowing look.

"Ok. I admit I wanted to get you into my bed and make my father angry. But one thing changed from that time, and one thing stayed the same. It changed that I love you so much if we compare it with our first encounter. But the thing that did not change is....I want you to get into my bed again and again. And these two will not change. Never." He confessed and winked at me.

"Pervert!" I exclaimed, laughing.

"But you are in love with this pervert."

"Yes, I am freaking crazy." I said.

"And freaking sexy." He added and brushed his lips against mine, kissing me passionately.

The End.

Thanks for reading, voting and commenting.

9 781787 990760